THE MYSTERIOUS ADVENTURES OF MARSHAL YEAGER, PROFESSIONAL ENGINEER - BOOK 1

THE MYSTERIOUS ADVENTURES OF MARSHAL YEAGER,
PROFESSIONAL ENGINEER - BOOK 1

In the Matter of:
SANDRA BULLOCK'S HOUSE,
GOVERNOR RICK PERRY,
AND CORRUPTION AT THE
TEXAS BOARD OF PROFESSIONAL
ENGINEERS

JUNE MELTON, III, P.E.

MARTIN & BYRD BOOKS, LLC • LAKEWAY
2010

Published in the United States by
Martin & Byrd Books, LLC
P.O. Box 342253
Lakeway, TX 78734

ISBN 978-0-9826519-1-9

Library of Congress Control Number: 2010903530

Printed in the United States of America

First Edition

Dedicated in memory of Mother and Dad, and my little sister, Linda.

Dedicated to the memory of Mrs. Courtney Dickson.

And dedicated to the youth of America,
who now hold the uncertain future
of our constitutional liberties
in their hands.

CONTENTS

1

❧ THE FALL OF BONFIRE ❧

Brittany Anderson laughed as her blond hair danced in the breeze across her nose and mouth. The eighteen-year-old swayed gently back and forth in her swing, gliding across the night sky. *What would Mom and Dad say to me if they saw me now*, she thought.

She stopped her swing from moving by stretching her leg and jamming her shoe against the top of a log. Her jacket had blown open, but the maroon jersey beneath was thick enough to keep her warm. Brittany dared not try to bring her jacket together and zip it up. *Not right now, I might fall!* she thought. She gripped her hands tightly to the two ropes that held her safe and kept her from falling.

Brittany looked downward beneath the glare of the lights directed toward her into the semidarkness below. She could see that she was about sixty feet above the ground. Her friends below were busy lifting logs and tying them together with pieces of wire. As she looked down, she instinctively grabbed the ropes tighter trying to remain as still as possible. Brittany precariously hovered above the top of the enormous log tower that formed the shape of a wedding cake.

She had not been particularly afraid of heights before, but as she focused on the busy students working below, she realized that if the rope carrying her swing happened to break or untie . . . *Well, I won't think about that right now.*

The glaring light shining from the spotlights below blinded her eyes. She turned her face away and then looked around, surveying the massive project. She could see several other students swaying in their swings nearby.

As she looked upward and studied the rigging of the ropes that held her swing, she could see that the two ropes in her hands were shackled to a single rope high above her that had been drawn through a pulley. The pulley was connected to a crosstie that extended out from the huge wood pole. She squinted her eyes, trying to see how the pulley was connected. "Looks sturdy enough," Brittany muttered hopefully.

She looked up to the top of the pole towering above her that was pointed to the sky. *The top of that pole has to be at least another thirty feet above me*, she thought.

Her gaze drifted to the quarter moon in the sky. It was a beautiful starry night. "The stars are so bright up here," she yelled to her friends below.

Another gentle gust of wind again caused her swing to move. She was next to the top of the fourth tier of logs of the 'wedding cake' tower. She again placed her foot on top of the log and sighed. Then she yelled, "I've had enough of this height! Would somebody please lower me down to the second tier?"

Another student loosened the rope from far below her, and Brittany began to descend downward toward the second tier of logs. A stronger gust of wind blew across her flushed cheeks. There was a sharp chill in the air. As the top of the second tier grew closer, she released her right hand and zipped her jacket tight. She pulled up her sleeve and looked at the watch that her mother and father had given to her as a high school graduation gift. It was 2:28 a.m. on the dark Thursday morning of November 18, 1999.

For most of her life, Brittany's father had talked about Texas A&M University. She heard countless stories of what it was like to be a Texas Aggie with the school's military traditions and the agricultural and engineering programs. Ever since she was a little girl she had watched football games with her father. And each year for as long as she could remember, he had taken her to see the stack of logs that the students built, and then burned, before every football game against their archrivals—the University of Texas Longhorns. The tradition had been ongoing at Texas A&M for almost a century.

By the time she entered high school, she had grown to love the camaraderie she had seen the Aggies display at the annual event called Bonfire. She wanted to experience that sense of solidarity for herself. Now here she was, a freshman at Texas A&M and living her dream, helping to build Bonfire and carry on the tradition.

Before this night, approximately 5,000 Texas A&M students and former students had invested over 125,000 work hours gathering old logs from nearby forests and hauling them to the Texas A&M campus to construct the Bonfire structure. As part of the tradition, more than fifty Aggie student organizations would plant trees to restore the environment the following spring.

In order to begin the construction of the center pole for the structure, a fourteen-foot deep hole had been drilled into the ground and a tall utility pole had been inserted with a large crane. Another utility pole had been spliced to the top of the lower one. When connected together the center pole towered over ninety feet above the ground. The Aggies had then attached crossties near the top of the pole to carry the swings.

At the beginning, Bonfire consisted simply of burning a pile of trash and having a pep rally around the fire before the football game. With time, students would lean wood logs against a center pole to form the shape of a teepee. Later, because a true teepee can only be built as high as the tallest log, multiple layers of logs had been added against and on top of each other before being set on fire. By the late 1960s, the height of the stack had grown to be over one hundred feet before being ceremoniously burned.

Eventually, the bonfires began to take on a more wedding cake–shaped appearance, containing up to six separate and relatively flat-top tiers of vertically stacked logs. A single tier would be built and the logs wired together. Successive logs would be spaced and individually wired to form a growing spiral at each tier. At all tiers, the logs would be stacked so that they would lean inward toward the center pole. The next tier would be built several feet smaller in diameter than the tier below. Then those logs would be wired together followed by construction of more tiers of logs.

Brittany's assignment had been to sit in the swing and help position each log at the fourth tier and then wire it to the other logs. She did not know that engineering plans had not been prepared for the Bonfire structure. She could not have known that the school administration and engineering faculty had spent years avoiding that fact. Brittany was just doing what she had been told to do.

By 2:30 a.m. she had been lowered in her swing to a position facing the top level of the second tier of logs. At this tier, she was still roughly thirty feet above the ground. About seventy other students and recent graduates were standing on the ground nearby or crawling over the upright logs, helping lift and stand additional logs upright and wire the logs together.

Suddenly, she saw the log in front of her move. Then she heard a loud thundering crack—the center pole had snapped. She looked up and saw the third and fourth tiers of logs starting to lean.

"Oh, God! It's falling!" she screamed.

2

☙ A LEGAL FIX ❧

Almost four years after the fall of Bonfire, a white 1998 Chevrolet sedan entered a parking garage in downtown Austin and pulled into a parking space. As both doors opened, a man climbed from the driver's side. He wore polished cowboy boots, well-worn blue jeans, and a western shirt with an open leather jacket. He had a tall, slender frame and a head full of gray hair. He reached in the backseat for his trusty western hat that made him look even more imposing.

The woman climbed from the passenger side of the Chevy. Her hair had once been blond, but now there were shiny sprigs of gray intermixed. She wore new blue jeans, a brown blouse, a denim jacket, and western boots. She was much shorter than her male counterpart. Both he and she had dark wrinkles around their eyes and across their foreheads that made them appear much older than their mid-40s.

On this day shortly before Halloween, it was unusually cold as a result of a Blue Norther that had blown in the night before. The pair walked down the stairs of the parking garage and exited onto the sidewalk of East Sixth Street. People were scurrying in both directions on the sidewalks. The man and woman turned left and walked along East Sixth. They bypassed the delivery workers carting liquor, beer, and food from delivery trucks to the various bars, restaurants, and music venues preparing for the annual adult Halloween street carnival to be held later that week.

They reached the corner of Sixth Street and Congress Avenue and saw their destination—the majestic Scarbrough Building that had been built in the early 1900s and was the first structural-steel skyscraper built in the capital city.

As the traffic light turned green, the pair crossed Congress Avenue and entered the building's lobby. They loosened their jackets, identified themselves to a stone-faced security guard, and then stepped into the elevator. The man then pressed the button that would take them to the top floor of the building—the ninth floor.

As the elevator arrived at its destination, the couple walked into the corridor. Glancing in both directions, they walked rapidly down the hallway, their boots clunking on the old polished terrazzo floor. They counted the metal office numbers fastened to the wide frames above each ancient wooden door. Finally they saw the number 930.

"Here it is," the man said, pointing to the lettering painted on the obscure glass framed into the upper half of the door. The lettering read "Marshal Yeager, Professional Engineer."

The man opened the door so that the woman could enter ahead of him. Inside the small reception area they saw a plump white-haired woman about seventy years old sitting behind a reception desk working at a computer. "Hello," the man said.

The receptionist looked up from her computer, took off her computer glasses, and asked, "May I help you?"

The man said, "We are Brittany Anderson's parents—John and Lucy Anderson. We called for an appointment to meet with Mr. Yeager. We're a little early."

The receptionist smiled and extended her hand. "I'm Myrtle. I'm Marshal Yeager's receptionist. I'm also his typist, secretary, assistant, computer technician, bookkeeper, and office janitor. I'm so glad to meet you both. Marshal told me about what happened to your daughter in that Bonfire tragedy four years ago. I'm so sorry. Please sit down. Marshal is in there and knows you're coming."

She pressed the button on her phone. "Marshal, your nine o'clock visitors are here a little early."

"Ask our visitors to wait, please. I'll be ready in a few minutes," the voice on the speaker boomed.

The Andersons sat on the leather sofa facing toward Myrtle, who had resumed working on her computer. Neither visitor picked up any of the magazines lying on the tables next to them. Both John and Lucy Anderson stared down at the polished hardwood floor.

Marshal Yeager had spoken from the other end of the speakerphone, but he was not in his office on the ninth floor. Instead, he was in his laboratory one floor below, accessible by a hidden spiral staircase that was contained behind an old wooden door that led from his office. This room was where he did his real work. The wood floor was unfinished. The plaster on the walls and ceiling were cracked and unpainted. The room was lined with file cabinets, bookcases, three work tables, three chairs, several desktop computers, a TV and DVD player, an old drafting table with a horizontal slide bar and screw-on lamp, an automatic drafting pencil sharpener, notepads, sandpaper, magnifying glasses, boxes of wax pencils, rubber bands, a drafting stool, and shelves filled with rows of boxes of computer software. A solitary slide rule hung on an accessible portion of a wall.

There were shelves littered with old specimens from previous forensic engineering cases that Marshal had investigated. Some specimens had paper tags affixed and some were in marked plastic bags. There were some broken electrical switches, a piece of wood with a metal strap from the site of a hurricane, small pieces of broken steel plate from a bridge collapse, pieces of rubber expansion joint material, pieces of pipe, bags of bolts and nails, some sand and clay specimens, a piece of broken skylight material, and a piece of a wood roof overhang taken from a house. One shelf contained about 50 movie DVDs, a stack of music CDs, and a CD player that softly hummed with the bluegrass fiddle and banjo music of the Onion Creek Crawdaddies.

Marshal was seated in an adjustable secretarial chair at the middle table reading documents. He was about six feet tall and the chair was set too high for the table, forcing him to lean over too far to read and causing his back to ache. He readjusted the chair while he continued to read.

He tried to squint through his wire rim glasses at some documents that he held in his hands. Marshal's eyesight had gotten worse over the years, and he found himself constantly readjusting the lower part of his bifocals to prevent them from sliding off his protruding nose. He was in his mid-sixties but still had a full head of hair that had started turning gray at the age of forty. He kept his hair cut and groomed neatly and businesslike. His chin was prominent, and his face had been clean shaven for many years. In his youth, he had allowed a mustache and beard to grow, but being outdoors in the Texas summer heat had taught him that he would be much more comfortable without facial hair. Besides, the facial hair had made him look like Abraham Lincoln.

He had answered Myrtle's page without looking up from the stacks of newspaper clippings, files, and computer-generated documents that he had been poring over since 4 a.m. As he searched through the documents on his table, he had perceived signs of dishonesty in the documents that he was reading. He had seen corruption many times before on individual, corporate, and government-agency levels, but it was the latter where he was focusing his attention this morning.

Marshal had spent his entire life since college working as a structural, civil, and architectural engineer, first as a beginning engineer with two different Houston engineering-construction companies and then with a medium-sized architectural firm. Then after he had acquired sufficient engineering experience on his resume, he had been able to qualify to take the engineering practices exam to become licensed as a professional engineer. After passing the exam, he had worked for several engineering consultants and had eventually broken free of the corporate life. He headed up his own architectural engineering design firm employing about twenty-five people. Eventually, he decided that the burdens of government regulation on small engineering corporations were too much for him. His hair had been turning gray from the stress. Even though he had loved his company and his employees, he had found himself miserable having to let many of them go during the recession of the 1980s. Despite the downturn, Marshal had still found a way to remain in business with five loyal employees who had remained with him to this day.

As a boy, Marshal had been fascinated by science shows on Saturday-morning TV shows. He had learned how to do simple science experiments in school. He had used his hands to build models of cars, airplanes, and electrical gadgetry including crystal radios and electric switches that would trigger an alarm when his younger sisters entered his bedroom. Marshal had also enjoyed building clubhouses and other things. He had not excelled in mathematics, particularly algebra, and although his parents had arranged for special tutoring and his grasp of algebra had improved, he continued to be an average student in mathematics. However, during Marshal's senior year in high school he had taken a college preparatory math course in which the teacher was so dedicated to the subject of mathematics and geometry—and the teacher's enthusiasm for mathematics rubbed off on Marshal to such an extent—that after graduation, Marshal was able to advance out of the first year of college mathematics and move on to a more advanced level.

Marshal had participated in competitive sports at school and would get into fistfights with bullies who would pick on the smaller kids. His leadership capabilities were instilled in him by his parents and also by his friends, many of whom had fathers who had fought in combat during World War II and who had instilled the sense of duty to America within their own children. His interest in the problems experienced by people of color evolved from the fact that his great uncle had been an Austin detective and also a Texas Ranger and had written how he was one of a group of lawmen who had tried to protect a defendant during a trial in Waco, Texas. His great uncle and the other lawmen, including the judge, had been overrun by a mob determined to lynch and burn the black man who was on trial.

Marshal's interest in political corruption had begun during his teenage years due to his father's warnings that the federal government would one day impose socialized medicine on the nation by controlling the insurance companies first. His father had been a surgeon, and he and Marshal had both recognized the stark, criminal nature of socialism, communism, and fascism. Marshal had always believed that engineers were the true environmentalists and rather than try to save the lives of people one by one like his father had done, he had considered becoming an engineer who would use professional skills to help a greater number of people all at once. When President John F. Kennedy inspired an entire generation of young people to study engineering by setting an example and pledging to put a man on the moon before the end of the 1960s, Marshal knew that engineering would be his future.

Ultimately, it had been his extensive engineering and business activities that had exposed him to the types of people who engaged in unsavory banking, business, and political interests. He had been exposed to many legitimate and illegitimate business practices in his life, recognizing that when people behave as individuals, most people will deliberately avoid the temptations of dishonest behavior that they know will get them into trouble. On the other hand, there were others he had met along the way who had enjoyed the excitement of ill-gotten gains and who were now in prison or were dead. He had also learned that when dishonesty manifests itself in the corporate or government bureaucracy setting, then the insular feeling of collective dishonesty lessens the ability for individuals to resist committing dishonest acts along with other members of the group. He had witnessed a small number of professional engineers take that dark path in life. They had been the ones who had deliberately sought unjustified compensation by receiving bribes from building contractors in return for certifying defective work as being acceptable.

His first exposure to corruption in the engineering, corporate, and political contexts was within a year after he had graduated from college with his master's degree. He had been employed as a junior engineer by Green and Arbor, a large engineering and construction firm in Houston. He had started in the marine sciences division, designing offshore oil drilling platforms. After a reorganization of that division, Marshal had transferred to the architectural/structural and civil engineering division where he had participated in the design of office buildings, warehouses, wastewater facilities, petroleum facilities, petrochemical plants, laboratories, government buildings, and domestic and foreign shipping ports. Lyndon Johnson was president of the United States at that time and Johnson's connections to Green and Arbor were well known throughout Houston. The young Marshal Yeager suddenly found that he was working as a company ambassador assigned the task of befriending many of Johnson's friends in Houston. Marshal had met with wives of Johnson's friends to design for them, free of charge, their kitchen remodeling projects and room additions. For Johnson's male friends, Marshal would design car garages, carports, boathouses, fishing piers, home workshops, and hunting cabins. Without Marshal's knowledge at the time, Green and Arbor would then construct, at no charge, the projects that Marshal had designed for Johnson's friends. In exchange, Marshal's new contacts, mainly wealthy Houston oil men, would persuade their friends to provide vast sums of money to Johnson who, Marshal was told, then reciprocated by seeing to it that Green and Arbor received large government contracts at taxpayer expense. For this and other reasons, Marshal then resigned from Green and Arbor.

Sitting now in his laboratory, a much older and wiser professional engineer, Marshal pushed aside those and other memories and finished gathering the documents he needed, tucked the documents under his left arm, climbed the spiral staircase, and entered his office on the ninth floor. He closed and locked the door behind him, tossed the documents onto his desk, grabbed his sport coat from the coat rack, and then opened his office door that led to the reception area. He stepped into the reception room and smiled broadly at the Andersons. Slightly out of breath from the climb up the stairs, he said, "Hello, Mr. and Mrs. Anderson. I am Marshal Yeager."

The Andersons stood up to meet the engineer. His manner of dress gave him what was termed an "Austin business casual" flair. He was dressed in a dark blue sport coat, brown slacks, and a patterned shirt with an open collar. His western boots were scuffed, indicating that he was not just an engineering office executive but that he was also away from his office on construction site inspections a great deal of his time. They could see that his wire rim glasses gave focus to his hazel eyes that were sharp and alert but also gentle. He exuded an air of confidence and determination—a decision maker.

After cordial exchanges, Marshal said, "John and Lucy, please come into my office."

The Andersons entered Marshal's large corner office. The tall ceiling transfixed the eye with its refinished dark brown inlaid hardwood and molding. The brass fan blades of two suspended antique wide-globe light fixtures sat motionless on this cold morning.

The wall plaster exhibited a light-colored faux finish and the floor was dark stained hardwood.

One exterior wall contained Marshal's desk area, and on each side of the desk were two large antique double-hung wood windows that drew the eye eastward up Sixth Street. The windows on the other exterior wall faced northward, providing a view of the Texas State Capitol building located several blocks farther north up Congress Avenue.

The walls of the office were adorned with pictures of buildings and bridges that Marshal had designed during his career. As John and Lucy had entered Marshal's office, they could see that on the wall to the left, separated by another door, were Marshal's architectural engineering degrees from the University of Texas. There were also his professional engineering licenses that had been granted to Marshal by various states as well as certificates of appreciation from various school groups for his financial contributions to the Math Counts, Destination Imagination, and industrial programs. Several office chairs and a leather sofa abutted the wall. A solid brass theodolite surveyor's instrument stood mounted to a brass tripod at the far corner of the room.

The wall to the right was lined with cabinets and a door adjoined by shelves full of books of many topics. There were books on engineering research, architecture, history, travel, politics, several classics, mystery stories, and novels.

"Those books are not just for decoration. I do make an effort to find time to read now and then," Marshal smiled.

On Marshal's large mahogany desk sat a single desktop computer with a Webcam, phone, and several thick manila folders. In front of the desk were two dark brown leather chairs resting on a large conservatively valued Mahi Persian rug. Behind the desk was a burnt orange executive chair, and behind the chair was a long mahogany credenza that abutted the wall. On top of the credenza were some engineering drawings and file folders containing documents. On the wall above the desk, between two of the east-facing windows hung two large G. Harvey western paintings.

Marshal motioned for the Andersons to take a seat in the two chairs in front of the desk. John and Lucy sat down in each of the chairs and Marshal sat in the executive chair. "Before we get started," Marshal said, "your lawyer told me what happened to your daughter, Brittany. Tell me, how is her health?"

"She's almost totally recovered," John said. "She has regained almost all of her mobility in her lower back. With future medical advances she will possibly be able to reach full mobility one day. She transferred to Texas Tech University after spending several months in the hospital after the Bonfire collapse. She is a senior now, majoring in civil engineering. She will graduate next year and is thinking about going on to the University of Illinois for her master's degree. Illinois is one of the best engineering schools in the country."

"I know," said Marshal. "I tried hard to get into the University of Illinois for my own master's studies program. From what your lawyer told me earlier, you might also encourage Brittany to consider a master's program in biomedical engineering at the University of Texas here in Austin. But I am very happy to hear that your daughter is doing so well. So tell me what happened to her the night of the Bonfire collapse."

John looked at his wife who said, "You tell him, John." John then said, "Brittany was sitting in a swing tethered by a rope from one of the crossties attached near the top of the center pole. She says she remembers seeing the stack of logs and the center pole leaning away from her, but that's the last thing she actually remembers. A young Aggie cadet came by the hospital and told us that he had seen the center pole collapse along with the log pile and had seen Brittany's swing, with Brittany still sitting in it, jerked high above the collapsing pile of logs as the pole leaned over and struck the ground away from her.

"Actually that's probably the thing that saved her life, because a split second after she was in the air, a portion of the stack also fell toward the side where she had just been sitting. Brittany was slammed down on top of one of the logs, fracturing her hip and lower spine. She was unconscious when they pulled her from the top of the stack, and they rushed her to the hospital. She was one of the twenty-seven injured. As you probably know, twelve of the other young people working on that Bonfire structure died that night or shortly thereafter. Several of them were Brittany's friends."

"She has had nightmares for years after that," Lucy added.

"Lucy and John, I assume your lawyer told you about me, right?" Marshal asked.

"Yes," said John. "He told us that most of the engineering work that you do is design work and also quite a bit of forensic engineering work that usually involves property owners and sometimes involves lawyers. He also said that you have investigated a lot of accidents from an engineering perspective and also various types of engineering failures related to construction projects. And as I'm sure you know, Bonfire was ruled by the Texas Board of Professional Engineers to be a construction project."

"As a point of clarification," said Marshal, "probably no more than twenty percent of the work that I do involves lawyers. Some engineers work for lawyers one hundred percent of the time, usually for defense lawyers, but some also do it for plaintiff lawyers. As you may know, there's a particular taint associated with engineers who testify a great deal. They develop reputations as 'hired guns,' 'advocates,' 'tell me what you want me to say' proponents, or terms much worse than those. So I deliberately take on no more than two or three cases a year in order to avoid that kind of taint on my reputation."

"What does an engineering expert witness do?" Lucy asked.

"Well," said Marshal, "an expert witness, who is an engineer like me, is really a type of detective who uncovers the causes of building failures or failures in design or construction that result in injury or loss of value. I apply mathematics, physics, and knowledge of how materials function in analyzing the cause of the failure. Engineering is more than a science, it is also an art, and the professional licensing of it forces me to be well aware of public safety. An expert witness must be willing to go into the courtroom and express himself or herself to a jury of people who are unfamiliar with engineering or construction methods but not come across as professorial or an intellectual snob. The expert witness must have many years of experience in his or her chosen profession; he or she must be unbiased, absolutely truthful, and not shape an opinion to fit the biases of the client or the client's lawyer. In my own case, my education, experience, and licensing are all in the field of professional engineering which is a multidiscipline practice, plus I am specialty licensed as an engineer in some states. I have the ability to think outside the box which some call 'forensic engineering.' In the role of expert witness, I have to think like a detective who is trying to solve a crime.

"When I am asked to investigate an engineering failure of some type as a consulting expert or testifying expert, I must be able to show that my knowledge of engineering is beyond that of the average person so that others can officially and legally rely upon my scientific opinion about an evidence or fact issue that is within the scope of my expertise. I can also deliver an expert opinion from the domain of my professional expertise."

"Let me tell you where we stand on the lawsuit," John said. "Our lawyer probably told you that I graduated from Texas A&M and also that I am not an engineer. After the Bonfire collapse that injured Brittany, I cut all my ties to Texas A&M. Some time back we decided to have our lawyer file a lawsuit against the university officials. He had already filed another lawsuit on behalf of the estate of a student who died in the collapse. The district court limited discovery in the case and then dismissed our claim along with all the others. Our lawyer has filed an appeal with the United States Fifth Circuit Court of Appeals, but it looks like the university might prefer to fight us rather than pay Brittany's extensive medical expenses. Meanwhile, we wanted to know your opinion about the report on the Bonfire collapse that was generated by the investigative engineers. Even if we lose at the Fifth Circuit, our lawyer believes that if you can uncover some new evidence, then he might have grounds to continue with our case."

Marshal reached into the stack of documents on his desk. Some of the documents had been sent to Marshal by the Andersons' lawyer.

"I have read the Special Commission Report that your lawyer sent to me," Marshal said. "It is apparent to me that the Bonfire stack collapsed due to poor construction and design practices made possible by a chronic lack of oversight from the university. The investigators found that over Bonfire's long history, it had evolved into what the report characterized as a 'complex and dangerous structure' that was allowed to be built without adequate physical or engineering controls.

"The report stated that during the tree-cutting and logging process, the students had found it difficult to find enough straight trees to cut down for Bonfire, so the students cut and then hauled more crooked logs than ever before. As the first tier was being stacked vertically and wired together, the crooked logs made it difficult to densely pack and tightly wire the stack together. Then while the second tier was being built, the logs on the second tier were inserted into the gaps between the logs on the first tier, creating a wedging effect. In previous years, because very few crooked logs had been used, there had been very few gaps that would have allowed the upper-tier logs to be inserted into the spaces between the lower-tier logs. During those previous years the logs had been simply stacked directly on the top surface of the logs below and then wired together.

"Also, in 1999 the students had stacked the logs much more vertically than before, instead of leaning them in the direction of the center pole. This arrangement increased the forces acting on the tie wires. Also at the second tier, more logs were stacked on one side of the center pole than on the other side, which created more stress on the lower stack. The heavy steel cables that had been used in earlier Bonfires to wrap the perimeter of each tier, similar to the steel hoops you see wrapped around the wooden slats of a rain barrel, were all left out. None had been installed before the log tower collapsed. The commission reported that the wiring provided the only source of hoop strength and was the first component of the Bonfire to fail under the mass weight of the logs that were stacked above. Vastly stronger wiring would have been required and restraining cables wrapped around each tier would have greatly reduced the likelihood of collapse.

"In addition to the physical engineering causal factors, the commission report also delved into behavioral factors that contributed materially to the collapse. The report cited a lack of a written Bonfire design or construction methodology as being very relevant to the collapse. The report noted that design decisions were made with no written guidance, no formal reviews, and no knowledge of critical design factors. In other words, there were no engineered plans for the students to work from. The report also criticized the university's risk management model and commented on a cultural bias that resulted in missed opportunities to identify structural problems.

"The report concluded the collapse was about physical failures driven by organizational failures, the origins of which span decades of administrations, faculty, and students. It concluded that no single factor caused the collapse and that 'no single change will ensure that a tragedy like this never happens again.'"

"So are you satisfied with the report?" John asked.

Marshal looked down, averting his eyes. He was trying to think of how best to answer the question. Finally he looked up and said, "No, I am not satisfied. Quite frankly, I believe that the report has serious flaws, particularly with respect to how it reported the actions of the engineering administration and faculty. Don't get me wrong. There were very intelligent and honorable people who worked on that report, some of whom I know professionally. But I am suspicious of several things related to how the report came together.

"First, I have no qualms about the mechanics of the failure as described by the engineers in the report. I thought the technical work that was generated by the engineers was very detailed and very professional. But then I had to ask myself, why would the engineers go to such detailed work and not place their professional engineering seals on the report after they had written it? That's a clear violation of the Texas Engineering Practice Act—an engineer must seal all plans and reports. Not doing so can mean that the engineer is not confident in his own report. But then I rationalized that maybe the copy of the report that your lawyer sent to me was not the official copy, and maybe the official copy does have the engineers' seals attached. So I've put that issue aside for now.

"Second, I am concerned about the way the investigation was managed. Shortly after the Bonfire collapse, the Texas A&M administration appointed several individuals to serve on an independent special commission to investigate the tragedy. The charter of the special commission was to determine what had caused the Bonfire to collapse and then issue a final report. At least two individuals were appointed to manage the investigation. Braker and Box, a Houston law firm, was also involved at the management level.

Have you ever heard of Braker and Box?"

"Yes," John answered, "but I don't know much about them."

"Think of former President George H. W. Bush and his presidential library at Texas A&M," Marshal said, "but I'll get into the political issue in a minute. I do think that the simple acknowledgment in the report of a law firm managing the engineers' actions does raise a red flag, as it should also raise a red flag to your lawyer. The commission report projects the image of a law firm controlling an engineering investigation and report. Whether or not that happened in this case, you should know that no lawyer is allowed to shape what a professional engineer puts in his or her report. It makes the engineer look like he is simply writing what the lawyer wants the engineer to write.

"Anyway, the commission organized several teams. One engineering firm focused on understanding and evaluating historical Bonfire designs. Another engineering firm investigated the physical aspects of the collapse, assisted by other engineers and technical experts. Additionally the commission engaged several outside engineers to provide peer reviews and comment on the engineering reports. Another team conducted an analysis of both past and present Bonfire organizational and behavioral issues, including conducting interviews, coordinating document and data collection, and investigating the effects of external factors on the Bonfire. According to the report, over 260 interview reports were analyzed. Interviews included eyewitnesses, current and former student leaders, and workers. Surveys were conducted of student workers. Over 4,800 separate documents including photographs, internal memos, newspaper accounts, and documents related to past Bonfire problems were compiled.

"Your lawyer told me that after the report was completed, the District Court then adopted the commission's final report pretty much as gospel and determined from that report that the actions of the university officials did not, as a matter of law, rise to the level of deliberate indifference. And as a result of that action, the district court dismissed the claims of those injured or killed."

"Yes, that's true," said John.

"One of the items in the report that caught my eye," said Marshal, "was a comment that one of the teams was assigned to interview university officials and engineering faculty who had previously expressed public concerns about Bonfire. I then decided to do a little research on my own, so I had Myrtle do research on the Internet and pull every relevant newspaper article she could find for the period of November 18, 1999, through 2000. What she found really bothered me.

"For instance, she found that one of the highest officials at Texas A&M, an engineer with bachelor's and doctoral degrees, had personally visited the Bonfire site several times before the collapse but said nothing to the students about the dangerous structure they were building. Also, the engineering faculty had tried over the years to warn the school administration that the design of the Bonfire contained perilous engineering design flaws."

Marshal stopped talking at that point. "I need some water. Can I get you some water or juice?" The Andersons shook their heads as Marshal stood up, walked over to a small refrigerator that was encased within the end of the credenza, and opened the refrigerator door. He pulled out a bottle of water and returned to his chair.

Marshal handed some newspaper clippings to the Andersons, still holding one clipping in his hand. "I'm going to hand you this particular article in a minute. It quotes members of the engineering faculty saying things like, 'We all have some regrets, now, that we kept quiet even though we thought it futile to speak up.' And 'many of the structural engineering faculty members were well aware of an unsuccessful attempt by one of the professors to have the design of the stack altered.' And it says, 'Several faculty members agree that the stack had been built in an unstable way in recent years.' This person says that an engineering professor had expressed the view for years that the stack design was 'fundamentally flawed' and had taken his concerns to the university's Office of the Vice President for Student Affairs and proposed a more stable design, but the 'university administration had ignored the recommendations.'"

Marshal now handed the clipping to the Andersons. He watched John and Lucy sitting quietly reading the newspaper clippings. He then poured his bottled water into a glass and drank. After a few minutes, they looked up after having read the clippings.

"I want to tell you a story that I think is relevant here," said Marshal. "The existence of laws dealing with the practice of engineering goes back to ancient times. The famous code of the Babylonian ruler Hammurabi who lived around 1800 BC, applied the 'eye for an eye' policy of enforcement toward engineering. The king said, 'If a builder erects a house for a man and does not make its construction firm, and the house which he built collapses and causes the death of the owner of the house, that builder shall be put to death. If it causes the death of the son of the owner of the house, they shall put to death the son of the builder.'

"In those days, the builder was also the engineer. Now I don't know if King Hammurabi ever had to see to it that an order to put an engineer to death was ever carried out, but after a while it was decided that society needed to be more civilized in how it treated its engineers, so the concept of the professional licensing of engineers eventually evolved. Actually, the concept of licensed professionals has been traced back to a decree made by King Roger II of Normandy in AD 1140. The decree required doctors to present proof of competency before being allowed to practice on the public. Professional competency was determined by passage of an examination and certification by a group of peers, much like professional licensing is done today.

"In the United States, the Tenth Amendment of the Constitution required the individual states to bear the responsibility for regulating the professions. The United States Supreme Court reinforced this requirement in the 1910 ruling of *Watson v. Maryland*. The decision addressed the licensing of physicians who, along with dentists and lawyers, had to become licensed in this country years earlier than engineers, in spite of the fact that engineers were required to adhere to more stringent education requirements than most of the other professions.

"In 1907, Wyoming became the first state in the nation to license professional engineers and land surveyors. Many incompetent people of that time who had benefited from the lack of standards resisted the new legislation, but it passed anyway. Other states began licensing engineers, but Texas held out licensing engineers for 30 more years. Then in 1937, a little girl named Mollie Sealey was sitting in a school bus in New London, Texas, waiting to be transported from the school auditorium to the gymnasium. Mollie saw the flash of an explosion as the school was lifted from its foundation and blown apart. Over 300 students and teachers died in the explosion. Later it would be determined that an electrical spark ignited an undetected gas leak. The explosion was attributed to faulty engineering.

"A few months later, nine-year-old Carolyn Jones who survived the blast but whose sister and uncle died in the explosion, appeared before the Texas Legislature and asked that children be protected from something like that from ever happening again. She said that parents should be able to send their kids to school and have them come back home safely. The Texas Legislature then created the Texas Engineering Practice Act and established the Texas Board of Professional Engineers.

"I find it highly ironic that so many parents lost their children in the Bonfire collapse at a public university in 1999, just like so many parents lost their children in the New London school explosion in 1937," Marshal said.

Lucy's eyes welled with tears, thinking of her daughter's injuries and all of Brittany's friends who had died that terrible day. The worry creases across Lucy's forehead had started to grow the very day she had gotten the news of the collapse. A friend had telephoned her, waking her at 4:30 that morning to tell her that Bonfire had collapsed and all they knew was that many students were dead. Her husband John had still been asleep. She had known that Brittany was to work on the Bonfire the day before. She was terrified for Brittany but also afraid that the shock of what might have happened to Brittany might kill John when she woke him to tell him what had happened.

Lucy looked at John and nodded that she was all right. "Marshal, please continue," said John, struggling quietly with his own worries about Lucy.

"One thing," said Marshal, "that sticks in the craw of a professional engineer is when he or she sees another engineer avoiding an engineer's statutory professional responsibility for the safety or welfare of the general public. The Texas Board of Professional Engineers is required by statute to protect the public from irresponsible engineers. The agency also has a requirement that engineers shall first notify involved parties of any engineering decisions or practices that might endanger the health, safety, property, or welfare of the public. When, in an engineer's judgment, any risk to the public remains unresolved, that engineer must report any fraud, gross negligence, incompetence, misconduct, unethical, or illegal conduct to the Board or to proper civil or criminal authorities.

"In other words, at a bare minimum under the law, professional engineers are required to report those kinds of engineers to the Texas Board of Professional Engineers, and I don't see that having happened in this case—at least as stated in the commission report that was apparently adopted by the district court.

"This gets me back to the commission's report. The people who performed the interviews of the engineering faculty members do not seem to have been engineers themselves. Under the law, people who are not engineers do not have to comply with this rule and report the engineers to the Board. Next, the engineers who comprised the engineering investigative team do not seem to have been in direct contact with the engineering faculty members so that they could personally interview them. If the investigating engineers were prevented from having direct knowledge of the actual behavior of the faculty members, then they had no obligation to report them to the Board. I think what we have here is a fundamental avoidance of responsibility, based on 'see no evil, report no evil.'

"Finally, we have the lawyers who were at the top of the management chain of command, and if they or the A&M administration happened to be predisposed to want a certain outcome that would protect the engineering faculty at Texas A&M, then what better way to accomplish that than to keep the engineering teams separated from the interviewing teams."

"Then you think the fix was in at Texas A&M?" asked John.

"Before I answer your question, I want both of you to be aware of a little more evidence that you can give to your lawyer," Marshal said.

3

☙ HIGH CRIMES AND MISDEMEANORS ❧

Marshal rose from his chair and crossed the office toward the shelves that contained many of his books. Pushing aside a copy of *Atlas Shrugged* by Ayn Rand, he finally found what he was looking for. He took a book from the shelf and opened it, searching for a particular section while he returned to his chair.

"This book is the Texas Engineering Practice Act and Rules concerning the practice of engineering," Marshal said to the Andersons. "Here is something I want to read to you:

> (a) The legislature recognizes the vital impact that the rapid advance of knowledge of the mathematical, physical, and engineering sciences as applied in the practice of engineering has on the lives, property, economy, and security of state residents and the national defense. (b) The purpose of this chapter is to: (1) protect the public health, safety, and welfare; (2) enable the state and the public to identify persons authorized to practice engineering in this state; and (3) fix responsibility for work done or services or acts performed in the practice of engineering. (c) The legislature intends that: (1) the privilege of practicing engineering be entrusted only to a person licensed and practicing under this chapter; (2) only a person licensed under this chapter may: (A) engage in the practice of engineering; (B) be represented in any way

as any kind of 'engineer'; or (C) make any professional use of the term 'engineer'; and (3) this chapter will be strictly complied with and enforced. (d) This chapter shall be liberally construed to carry out the intent of the legislature.

"Notice the words, 'fix responsibility for work done.' Those words can strike fear into everyone involved, apparently including the agency staff of the Texas Board of Professional Engineers, if the agency is under political pressure from outsiders.

"Based on my experience, many people who construct things that harm people have avoided responsibility for their actions ever since the New London school explosion in 1937 and enactment of the law. Back then, there was an intense lobbying effort by numerous special interest groups at the Texas Legislature. They wanted to be exempt from the new law that involved engineers so that they could carry on with their reckless practices same as before. They believed that having a licensed professional authorized by the state to design structures that would include enough materials to make the buildings safer could also make their buildings and other structures more expensive, and therefore profits would be harmed. Besides, hiring professional engineers might be expensive.

"Even now, the law still exempts almost everyone involved in construction projects, including homebuilders; apartment builders with some limitations on building size; garages, farm, and ranch structures; single-story buildings depending on size and type; and here's a particularly interesting one, to an engineer at least, that says a building is exempt if it 'does not contain a clear span between supporting structures greater than twenty-four feet on the narrow side.' That one came from an intense lobbying campaign by builders and owners of property in downtown Austin back in 1937. The downtown lots are generally twenty-five feet wide, and there were no building setbacks back then. So by the time the builders placed the walls of a building against each side property line, and subtracted about eight inches of masonry wall on each side to hold up the roof, then they had a clear span for the roof structure of less than twenty-four feet, which meant that they did not have to comply with the new Engineering Practice Act. It's still that same way today, and I have been told that is one reason that standard lumber lengths are limited to twenty-four feet.

"Let's see here, in the Act we also have others who are exempt from the law, including officers and employees of the United States Government; equipment installation mechanics and operators including train locomotives, steam engines, refrigeration equipment, communication equipment, and the like; small public works projects; large industries like refineries and petrochemical plants designing improvements for their own property; manufactured products; scientists and geologists; licensed architects; interior designers . . . Oh! Here, this is what I was looking for—'employees of institutions of higher education.'

"As I recall, engineering faculty have had the responsibility of becoming licensed as professional engineers since the early 1970s. You probably did not know that earlier this year, the Texas Legislature made employees of institutions of higher education exempt from the state requirements. Engineering faculty no longer have to be licensed, meaning they no longer have to be legally or ethically concerned about any engineering advice they give their students or anyone else.

"Guess who signed that legislation into law? Governor Rick Perry! Perry attended Texas A&M University where he had been a member of the Corps of Cadets and had also been one of A&M's male cheerleaders who are called 'yell leaders.'"

"Could Governor Perry have wanted that law changed to try to prevent us from filing suit against the various members of the A&M engineering faculty?" asked John.

"It's possible," Marshal said, "but you need to get with your lawyer on that. Governor Perry also signed into law an exemption for the National Aeronautics and Space Administration that permits NASA to employ unlicensed engineers. Do you remember that back in 1986 the NASA engineers tried to prevent the Space Shuttle *Challenger* from launching because of the effect that the cold weather would have on the 'O-ring seals,' but the business interests at NASA thought it would cost too much money to delay so they launched *Challenger* anyway? Seven members of the crew, including Christa McAuliffe who was part of NASA's Teacher in Space Project, died in that explosion. Now it looks like the corporate profiteers, with Rick Perry's help, are doing their level best to prevent professional engineers from speaking up. If engineers are not licensed and are under the control of the large corporations and universities, those engineers have no legal or ethical obligation to concern themselves professionally in protecting the health, safety, or welfare of the public. It's all about money and lack of responsibility.

"Let me walk you through what happened at the state level after the Bonfire collapse. Less than a month after the collapse, on December 10, 1999, the interim executive director of the Texas Board of Professional Engineers announced that the Board intended to investigate if Texas A&M University and its administration had violated the law by their failure to involve professional engineers in the project. The Board also intended to investigate if the engineers on the faculty had ignored their ethical duty by failing to raise concerns about the Bonfire structure over the years.

"On May 2, 2000, the special commission issued its report that included the analysis of the technical issues involved in the collapse but did not mention the obligations of the individual faculty engineers toward the health, safety, and welfare of the general public. On June 15, 2000, the Texas Board of Professional Engineers announced that the 'giant, six-tiered log tower amounted to a complex construction project that should be regulated by state engineering laws.' The Board's executive director stated, 'The commission's finding convinced the state agency that the bonfire was within its jurisdiction. The report clearly stated that it's a complex structure that lacked engineering controls.' In addition, with regard to the engineering faculty, the executive director said, 'The Board could also reprimand or revoke the licenses of A&M faculty engineers who had ignored their ethical duty under the law and had failed to raise warnings about the unsafe structure.'

"The Board's final inquiry was scheduled to be completed by September 2000. That month came and went. There was nothing but silence from the Texas Board of Professional Engineers. Do you remember what was happening here in Texas in late 2000?"

"I do remember the Bush versus Gore presidential election that year," Lucy said.

"That's right," said Marshal. "In late 2000, Rick Perry assumed the office of Governor of Texas when George W. Bush resigned the office to prepare for his presidential inauguration. As the new unelected governor of Texas, Perry began changing members of Texas agency boards and commissions, although it was about 2002 when he began changing the members of the Texas Board of Professional Engineers. Nevertheless, there have been signs that at least one of the members appointed by Governor Bush was doing Governor Perry's bidding even before 2002.

"On October 24, 2001, Dallas lawyer Steven DeWolf filed suit on behalf of the family of Christopher Breen, one of the students who died in the Bonfire collapse. DeWolf alleged that Texas A&M University and five top officials knowingly put Breen and others working on Bonfire in danger. That suit was styled *Sean Breen, et al., v. Texas A&M University, et al.* Darrell Keith, a Fort Worth lawyer, also filed suit on behalf of several other students. According to this article I have here, Keith said, 'What I call the Aggie Nation is a very close-knit group, which in large part considers itself above the law in my opinion. They are very resentful of anyone outside the A&M family seeking to hold them accountable for their wrongful conduct.'

"Then later, on July 26, 2002, the Texas Board of Professional Engineers and Texas A&M University entered into an 'Agreement of Voluntary Compliance' ensuring that any future Bonfires held on University property would require the employment of a professional engineer to draw plans and specifications. The then-executive director of the Texas Board of Professional Engineers said:

> Texas A&M and the engineering board agreed that if the Board brought an administrative action against the university in connection with the collapse, there would be significant legal and factual issues concerning whether the engineering board has legislative authority to take action against Texas A&M as a result of the bonfire collapse.

Because the university is willing to assume responsibility and comply with the Texas Engineering Practice Act for any future bonfires, we believe that it is in the public interest to accept Texas A&M's voluntary compliance rather than take administrative action against the university, considering the uncertain outcome and high cost to the state.

"So reading that, I wondered, 'What is the Board doing, talking about disciplining a public university? By state law, the Texas Board of Professional Engineers disciplines professional engineers as individuals. The Board does not discipline universities.' But with regard to the individuals involved, here is what I found in that agreement:

After the collapse, the engineering Board conducted an investigation to determine whether Texas A&M or any of its officials should be disciplined by the Board for failure to have a professional engineer design and supervise the construction of the bonfire stack. The university maintained that decisions regarding stack design or placement of the logs were made by students and volunteers who worked on the bonfire and its involvement was limited to matters unrelated to the planning, designing, organizing, and construction of the bonfire.

"In my opinion," Marshal said, "in that particular paragraph the Texas Board of Professional Engineers has ignored its obligations to the victims and the families of the young people hurt or killed by cutting a deal with Texas A&M that would allow the Board to avoid focusing on the irresponsible behavior of the people who had looked the other way while they had let the students make their own mistakes. In other words, Texas A&M and the Texas Board of Professional Engineers have together agreed that it's all the kids' fault that they got hurt or killed and none of the engineering faculty are to blame—at least that's what I believe that they are saying here. The only person in Texas with the power to put pressure on the Texas Board of Professional Engineers to get them to agree to that level of irresponsibility is the governor."

John's face grew red with anger. He was thinking about his daughter. He was thinking of when she had been a child and how she had depended on Lucy and him to take care of her. He was thinking about how worried they had been when they sent her to grade school, and then to high school where some drug-crazed kid might burst into her classroom with a gun and shoot her, and how he had depended on the school authority to protect her. And finally when she makes it to college, surrounded by dozens of older, seemingly intelligent and responsible faculty members and administrators, she becomes maimed by their total and absolute disregard for responsibility. And now here's a state governmental agency that is supposed to protect the public, exhibiting the same level of disregard and irresponsibility.

Marshal rose up out of his chair and walked slowly to the north window of his office. He stared out the window toward the Texas Capitol building and folded his arms across his chest. Without turning toward John and Lucy, he asked, "John, you were once an Aggie. You remember the Aggie Code of Honor, right?"

John regained his composure and then answered, "Yes I do. 'An Aggie does not lie, cheat or steal, or tolerate those who do.'"

Marshal stared at the Capitol and said, "John, I would like for you and Lucy to go back to your lawyer and tell him that I do believe that a fix was in with the preparation of the commission's report, with the purpose being to save Texas A&M from having to pay money to the families of the kids who died or were injured. Tell him that I would be more than willing to testify to that fact."

Still staring at the Capitol, Marshal said, "I also want you to tell your lawyer that I believe that there was also a fix that may have originated at the office of the governor—an office currently occupied by the Aggie-in-chief himself—the honorable Governor James Richard 'Rick' Perry of Texas."

4

♋ More Than Just a Plumbing Leak ♌

Near the end of 1999, as the nation was about to enter into a new millennium, there were fears that the anticipated Y2K computer bug might shut down banks, telephone companies, and government functions including the Social Security system. Some people filled the gas tanks in their cars and stocked up on survival manuals, food, and water. The government printed extra cash to distribute to panicked depositors who might storm the banks demanding their money as soon as the electricity and the computers shut down. But when the clocks struck midnight on New Year's Eve bringing the end to 1999 and the beginning of the year 2000, nothing unusual seemed to have happened. No trains stopped running on their tracks, and no planes fell from the sky. The Y2K computer bug had turned out to be a dud.

As 'bugs' go, Marshal Yeager was spending the advent of the new millennium in bed, suffering from the flu bug. He was unaware that movie actress Sandra Bullock had appeared on a late-night television show, discussing her new lake house that she was building in Austin and that a plumbing leak had appeared during a millennium party held at the house.

Five months later, in May 2000, just as Sandra Bullock was starting to move into her new house, the telephone rang on Myrtle's desk at Marshal's office. She answered and then said, "Yes, Dale, he's here. I'll transfer you." Pressing a button, Myrtle transferred the call to Marshal, who was working at his desk.

"Marshal, it's your old friend and client Dale Morgan on the phone."

Marshal switched on his headset as he leaned back in his chair. "Good morning, Dale. What are you doing on this beautiful spring day?"

"I've got an owner who wants an engineer to investigate a plumbing leak in a new house," Dale said.

"Dale, I've got projects going out the kazoo. You don't need an architectural engineer just to find a plumbing leak. Have the owner call a plumber."

"Marshal, it might be more serious than a simple plumbing leak. You might have to do a full due diligence inspection of the house— and it is a large house. You are the best engineer I know for this situation."

Marshal laughed, but Dale had piqued his interest. Dale was a commercial real estate broker with many business contacts throughout Texas. Over the years, Marshal had learned that whenever Dale had tried to flatter him into doing a project, it had turned out that Dale had already involved himself in an unusual situation and that involvement had led to Marshal learning a great deal more about how business was being conducted in central Texas. As the conversation continued, Marshal realized that Dale was not going to tell him anything more about the exact nature of the problem. Even more unusual was that Dale wouldn't even tell Marshal the name of the owner of the property he was asking Marshal to inspect. Finally Marshal said, "OK. I'll bite. I'll do it. Let's meet at the property. Tell the owner it shouldn't take too long."

On the appointed day, Marshal drove his refurbished, red 1964-1/2 Mustang convertible to the address that Dale had given him. Marshal stopped at a huge, opaque steel gate that blocked the road. Dale had not given Marshal a security code to use to open the gate, so Marshal stared at the security cameras that he saw were mounted on the fence to guard the gate.

In a few moments the gate began to slowly roll open, creating an opening on the right side. Marshal could see that the gate was mounted on steel rollers and steel railroad tracks. After opening about two feet, the gate suddenly jerked to a stop, apparently jammed. *Not too impressive*, Marshal thought.

Marshal moved his Mustang to the side of the road and got out of the car. He slung his camera bag over his shoulder, grabbed his notepad, and entered the opening. As he passed through the opening, he looked at the edge of the gate and along the back face of it. He wrote, "Deathtrap gate. No safety edge. Appears to be powered by a motor attached to a chain not much larger than a bicycle chain. Chain broken, lying on the ground."

As Marshal turned away from the gate, he tripped on something sticking up from the gravel driveway. It was a flexible polypropylene geotextile material that had evidently been installed to try to stabilize the soil underneath the gravel so that cars could drive over it. Marshal wrote on his pad, "Tripping hazard—geotextile protruding at driveway."

The house loomed upward about 150 feet to his right. It was large but seemingly compact at the same time. It was a tall two-story house with combination French- and English-style gothic architecture with stone veneer, large windows, turrets, several chimneys, and an arch-shaped tile roof. The house had been constructed several hundred yards from the western shore of the Lake Austin portion of the Colorado River that flows through Austin. The tract of land appeared to be about ten acres in size, with the middle and eastern portions of the site gently sloping to the lake with native grass and an abundance of large, old pecan trees that shaded most of the eastern portion of the property. The western section of the site, to Marshal's left as he walked along the driveway, featured a rocky, steeply sloped topography.

An old single-story, wood-frame farmhouse stood near the western slope, several hundred feet to the left of the driveway. It had obviously been recently remodeled into a guesthouse. The exterior walls exhibited some stone veneer but were mostly sided with white-painted original wood. Then one of the doors opened, and Marshal could see that it was Dale standing in the doorway. "Marshal, we're meeting over here in the guesthouse," Dale shouted.

Dale Morgan was about five feet, ten inches—slightly shorter than Marshal with brown hair, medium build, and clean shaven. He was in his early forties. Dale wore a golf shirt, dress slacks, and casual shoes. Marshal was wearing his tweed jacket, green slacks, and scuffed boots. The two men entered the kitchen where a woman was standing on the other side of the table. Dale introduced the woman as Ms. Hendrickson. Marshal perceived from Ms. Hendrickson's dark suit, tie, brown pulled-back hair, glasses, briefcase, and her demeanor that she was a lawyer.

Ms. Hendrickson spoke first. "Mr. Yeager, I am glad that you could come. Dale told us about you. He also gave us a copy of your resume. We are impressed."

"Thank you for your compliment, Ms. Hendrickson," Marshal said. "Please call me Marshal. Who are 'we'?"

"Marshal," Ms. Hendrickson said, "I represent Sandra Bullock's trust, and as you can imagine there are several people who work for Sandra. I am her trustee on this house construction project. We asked Dale not to tell you any details about this assignment until we could speak with you first. First off, throughout the duration of your investigations, we want you to keep details of your visits confidential. While Sandra was off making a movie, I was responsible for making sure that all bills sent to us by the house builder were correct and properly documented so that they could be paid. The builder had gotten Sandra involved in a 'cost-plus' contract, and we had been paying the building company, or 'builder' in this instance, on a regular basis as the work was being done. We had grown concerned because the builder had said the house was finished and was still working on punch-out items, but the builder has not been providing us proper backup information with the invoices. Now Sandra is in the process of moving some of her possessions into the house, but we have decided not to close out the contract with the builder until we straighten out the accounts."

"How much was the house supposed to cost?" Marshal asked.

"One and a half million dollars," Ms. Hendrickson replied.

"What's the total bill?" Marshal asked.

"Three to four million and still counting. Our auditors have been trying to get financial and other documents from the builder for many months now. The construction portion of the contract provided that the builder be paid on a cost-plus basis covering the actual costs of all necessary materials, labor, management, overhead, and insurance plus a fee of 15%. We discovered that the invoices that the builder had submitted for payment substantially exceeded the amount shown in the cost breakdown that was stipulated in the agreement, and much of the supporting documentation necessary to show the actual costs that had been incurred was not provided. Tell me, Marshal, what do you know about cost-plus contracts?"

"A cost-plus arrangement," Marshal replied, "between a builder and an owner requires the builder to use its best efforts to secure the best price available and to document all costs that it incurs. A contract needs to be carefully drafted in that manner. There are all kinds of possible irregularities that can occur in any cost-plus construction project, such as actual labor costs not paid at the rate billed to the owner; actual costs of contract work being less than the bid or proposal from various suppliers and subcontractors; cash paid back by the supplier to the contractor in an off-the-record transaction; material returned to a supplier not credited to the owner's project; owner being charged for non-cost items; materials, supplies, machine rentals, and subcontractor costs that are billed to the owner but are actually used on other projects; subcontractors required to buy back materials that are not consumed on the project but are billed to the owner; rebates or credits not given to the owner; phantom labor costs charged to the owner; payment of advances that are not deducted from later billings . . . I could go on and on, but it's beginning to sound like what you really need to do is retain a forensic accountant with specialized knowledge in construction accounting."

"Marshal, that's not why you are here," Ms. Hendrickson replied. "We've been speaking with a city inspector plus an additional inspector, whom the city terms a 'third-party inspector.' Both of them tell us that they think the house is unsafe, and the City of Austin does not want to sign off on it as being finished. We want you to inspect the house for yourself and tell us if it is all right for Sandra to start moving in her things. As you will see, she has already started to occupy the house."

"How did she get involved in this?" Marshal asked.

"As I'm sure you know, Sandra is an actress," Ms. Hendrickson said. "She had previously arrived in Austin to make a movie. Austin has a reputation as a music, arts, and entertainment center with a small number of moviemaking enterprises. She enjoyed the laid-back lifestyle here as compared to Los Angeles. Sandra decided to build her dream house in Austin. She found this particular beautiful tract of land where we are now. She attended a socially upscale party in Austin and was approached by a real estate broker who suggested that Sandra have a particular architect design and also build her dream house. There have been some issues involving that broker, but I won't bother you with that. The architect served as building designer, and he also owned or was a part of a construction company.

"When you meet Sandra you will realize that she is not the kind of person that many people think Hollywood represents. In other words, she is basically a normal and decent human being, and I think that's a personal quality that her fans recognize. Sandra became the architect's client, and like many young women who work with an architect to design their dream house, Sandra had clipped articles and pictures out of various magazines to depict what she wanted in her new house. She had gone into extensive detail describing her dreams to the architect and had trusted him to exercise his professional skills in transcribing those dreams to plans and specifications.

"When Sandra saw the architect's final drawings, she was understandably thrilled. But she had no way of knowing that the plans themselves did not depict a house that could be properly constructed. The construction project started badly. For example, although the architect was aware of the large number of trees on the site, he failed to prepare an existing tree layout on the site plan, properly dimensioned with respect to where the house was going to be placed. The house was shown on the site plan to be too close to the lake and within the grove of the largest pecan trees, which would require their removal.

"It was Sandra herself who discovered the error in the plans when a construction worker began to mark large trees for removal so that the foundation could be started. The foundation location was then moved farther away from the lake, but the appropriate changes were not made to the plans. Eventually the foundation was installed at too low of an elevation with respect to the ground. During the construction, water flooded into the house from the western slope. The builder then excavated a large portion of the yard in front of the house, below where the driveway is located, in an effort to get drainage to flow around the house. Then things really got worse as the project continued. You need to see inside the house and look at the poor-quality workmanship. But the workmanship is all that we can judge by. We need you to tell us if something is really wrong."

"All right, Ms. Hendrickson," Marshal said. "I'll look at it and take Dale with me. We'll be back in about an hour."

Marshal and Dale left the trustee at the guesthouse, crossed the driveway, and entered the front door of the main house. As they entered the main family room, Marshal asked, "Why do the French doors that face toward the lake have ropes tied around the door handles?"

"Because the doors are warped, the latches don't work, and you have to stand on a ladder to unlatch them at the top of the door," Dale said. "The security alarm keeps going off."

"Then how are you supposed to get out during a fire?"

"Go through the windows," Dale responded.

"What's this about a plumbing leak?" Marshal asked. They then walked to an area of the hallway near the kitchen. Marshal saw that dark water stains had streaked down the wall and had stained the already-finished wormwood flooring. He could see that the leak evidently originated from a bathroom on the second floor. The paint on the wall had buckled below the leak.

That looks repairable, Marshal thought to himself, *but why did it happen in the first place?*

As Marshal walked through the house, he was surprised to see such low-quality workmanship at the kitchen and bathroom cabinets, with irregular gaps visible as if the cabinet doors had been manufactured too small or had been hung on the cabinet openings haphazardly. He had seen better-quality workmanship in many of the least-expensive houses he had inspected in Austin, Waco, and San Antonio.

"Look at how rough this paint job is," Marshal said as they entered the large master closet. "Was there a sandstorm the day they painted these shelves and cabinets?"

"No," Dale replied, "That's painted sawdust. They were sanding the wood floors and also painting the walls and cabinets at the same time. The painting subcontractor told me that the builder was going to charge Sandra extra for sanding down the shelves and redoing them."

"Tell you what, let's save the cosmetic issues for later," Marshal said. "I want to look inside the attic and see if there are any problems with the roof structure."

Marshal climbed the pull-down stair that had been installed in the ceiling at a second-floor closet. He stepped into the dimly lit attic. Finding the switch, he turned on the lights. As he started to reach for his camera located inside the camera bag on his shoulder, he suddenly stopped, riveted to his position, staring into the now-lighted void.

He was not standing in a typical residential attic. He found himself standing in a dangerously unbraced attic. He was not looking at what most homeowners see inside the attics of their own houses, which is usually an arrangement of wood rafters or trusses that form the structural shape of a triangle or gable. Engineers regard the three members of a triangular shape to be connected together with frictionless pins or nails, and the triangle shape is the only stable plane-geometry shape there is. Quadrangles, pentagons, hexagons, and other shapes are not basic structurally stable shapes. In this house, the rafters had been installed by the framing carpenters in a manner that for the most part exhibited no structural triangulation whatsoever. Marshal was staring at a series of wood hexagons that formed the roof-frame shapes, with the flat portion of roof being approximately eleven feet high at the middle, with weak joints connecting the rafters together. The rafters would inevitably collapse if the wind reached an adequate velocity.

As Marshal placed his hand on one of the rafters while moving to another position, he felt the roof shake at the same time that he heard a loud "thump," as if someone had dropped a bowling ball on the roof overhead. The structure had suddenly shifted slightly and had then stopped while Marshal had been standing there. He saw that the entire roof section at that end of the house had already begun to lean in a direction toward the front of the house, and a portion of the roof over his head appeared to have sagged about two inches. He realized that the roof was exhibiting the early characteristics of a progressive structural collapse.

"I'm going to have to install movement monitors in this area," Marshal said out loud to Dale who had entered the attic by that time. "If this structure is moving back and forth with the wind, as I suspect it is, I need to record it with some gauges."

Working his way back to the attic access where he had first entered, he saw gaps in the attic-exposed portions of the chimneys and said, "If someone builds a fire in the fireplaces, there is the possibility that hot embers could escape into the attic space."

Marshal saw exposed wiring that could electrocute someone inside the attic. He also saw numerous water stains on the wood attic members that were obviously the result of a leaking roof.

"What an irresponsible waste of good materials," Marshal said. "This attic is going to require a lot of effort to repair."

Marshal and Dale exited the attic and walked back to the guesthouse where they met again with the trustee.

"Ms. Hendrickson," Marshal said, "there are serious issues inside the attic, but I need to do further investigation. I would like to come back in a few days when I have more time and can take some photographs so that I can show you what's happening rather than try to put it all into words."

Marshal wondered how such poor framing workmanship could have been approved by the city inspectors.

"I need your permission to interview some of the people at the City of Austin and also the builder's subcontractors," Marshal continued. "I would also like to obtain all written documents, including plans and specifications. Oh, one last thing. Do *not* let Sandra Bullock move into that house."

"What if she insists?" Ms. Hendrickson asked.

"That's between you and her," Marshal said. "Without alarming her, tell her I think the house has serious structural issues, but I've really got to get more evidence before I can make a final determination." He paused and then said, "Of course you can always tell me that you don't require my engineering services any longer. But please keep in mind that it is my understanding that you did ask me out here to tell you the truth."

Ms. Hendrickson then authorized Marshal to begin the investigation in earnest. She reiterated that Sandra's team had been unable to get important documents from the builder for several months. They had not even been able to get a complete set of plans and specifications and other construction documents.

"I've got a bad feeling about this project," said Dale. "I do know several people who were involved with the construction process, and I'm convinced that we had better move fast to get those documents. Ms. Hendrickson, most likely the financial records you can't get are in the builder's office but the construction documents, plans, specifications, and vendor and supplier information are in another location."

Based on what Marshal had already heard and seen, he too was already suspicious of the project and of the participants in the construction process. After the two men left the guesthouse, Marshal told Dale, "I'm not going to ask you how you intend to get those documents. Just make sure you do it fast, today if possible, and you do it legally. I don't want any evidence destroyed before you can get to wherever you need to go to get the stuff, and I don't want to have to bail you out of jail."

"Don't worry," Dale said. "It's legal."

"One more thing," said Marshal. "You've known me for a long time. You know that I have a reputation for tenacity and others know that, too. Does the builder know that I am involved?"

"No, not yet," said Dale, "but he will find out soon enough. His superintendent drove up a little while ago while we were talking in the guesthouse, and he is sitting over there in the main house watching us through that window. He probably got the license number off your car. The builder's not going to like you one bit."

Marshal replied, "That's interesting to hear. I'm going to need you to help me find out all of the reasons why he's not going to like me."

5

❧ A Slip of the Pen ❦

The septic system official at the City of Austin sat behind his desk, staring at the letter. It bore the name and signature of Arthur Borgenson, P.E.

"Arthur Borgenson is dead," the official said, his neck spilling over his necktie and his too-tight collar. He handed the letter back to Marshal.

"I'm sorry to hear that," Marshal said, "but then the question becomes how could Arthur Borgenson have signed a final engineering certification letter for the septic system located at Sandra Bullock's house when the septic system has still not been completed?"

"Let me see that letter again," the official said. Marshal handed him the letter and also handed him a copy of a final certificate of occupancy letter that had been granted by the City of Austin that Marshal had discovered in the city files.

By then, Marshal had greatly expanded his investigation of the Bullock house since first meeting with Ms. Hendrickson, the trustee at the guesthouse. Over a period of two weeks, he had returned to the site and had conducted several additional inspections, taking notes, making measurements, and taking over 300 photographs of deficiencies he had found. Marshal had seen to it that Sandra Bullock view those photographs and judge for herself if she should continue moving in. When she saw the photographs, she agreed to delay indefinitely her move into the house.

Marshal had accumulated enough information to persuade the trustee to allow him to hire other technical experts, including electrical engineers, geotechnical engineers, roofing specialists, environmental hazard specialists, plumbing and air ventilation specialists, and others who would be able to contribute their technical skills to conducting the necessary forensic investigations of the house so that they could write their own reports.

The investigation was to be kept confidential, and no one was to know whose house it was because Marshal did not want any of his experts to reflect any form of bias in any of their reports. He had given all of the experts only the address of the house where they were to do their work and had repeatedly emphasized that they were not to speak to anyone other than him about what they were discovering. When they asked Marshal who the house belonged to, he told them that he was not authorized to say anything about that.

Then one day while Marshal and his electrical engineering consultant were working at the house, Sandra arrived in a black Chevy Blazer to remove the rest of her belongings. She was dressed like one of the janitorial crew and was wearing dark glasses and a floppy hat that partially covered her face. Despite the disguise, the electrical engineer recognized her right away saying, "Hey, isn't that Sandra Bullock?"

"Yes," Marshal replied. "But keep it quiet, don't tell anyone else, and don't ask her for an autograph. If you're enamored with movie stars, think about a movie star closer to our ages. Do you remember Sandra Dee?"

"Sure do," said the electrical engineer. "I grew up in L.A. I never met her, but I wrote her a letter anyway and invited her to my high school senior prom."

"Bobby Darin probably told her to tell you no," Marshal laughed. "Otherwise, I don't think I want to hear any more about how that turned out. Let's get back to work."

It had been the electrical engineer who discovered that much of the electrical wire used in the house was of substandard gauge for the electrical load it was intended to carry, leading to his concerns that overheated wiring would probably cause a fire. He had also raised the issue of substandard wiring leading to the pump tank located adjacent to the septic tank. That's when Marshal had called the city and had learned that the septic system had been certified as being complete by Arthur Borgenson, the professional engineer who had designed the septic system very early in the construction process. Marshal then found the certification letter in the City of Austin files. Although the letter was stamped "original" in red ink with a city stamp, the text, signature, address, and other information appeared to be copies. This indicated that the document might have been copied from another project involving Borgenson, altered by an unknown person, and then copied and sent to the city.

Marshal found several certifications in the city files that made little sense. The engineer's septic system certification letter had been one of them. Another was an engineer's inspection letter certifying that reinforcing steel placement was being approved on a date that another document indicated had not yet started. Marshal then asked a lawyer at the city attorney's office to take possession of all of the city's Bullock house inspection files. The files had been accessible to the public, and Marshal worried that anyone could remove the documents and walk out of the building with them.

While reviewing the files, Marshal discovered that someone had submitted Borgenson's certification letter to the City of Austin in January 2000. Then in March 2000, someone with the city had issued a final certification of occupancy for the house. That same day, a remodeling permit had been taken out on the same property. A few days later, someone at the city had released a stop-construction work order on a retaining wall, two years after the retaining wall had already been completed on the property, which appeared to mean that the city's order had been ignored by a contractor. Then right in the middle of Marshal's investigation, someone at the city had issued a certificate of occupancy letter that could, in effect, authorize Sandra Bullock to move into her new, dangerous house.

The city septic system official read the certificate of occupancy and compared the date with the date of Borgenson's certification.

"Something is very wrong here," the official said. "Arthur Borgenson's letter is one thing, but so is the final city certification of occupancy. There's a complete process set up here. We've found that the new septic systems being installed nowadays are high quality and environmentally friendly, and no house in Austin that is served by a septic system can be occupied until this office approves the construction. We're the last step in the process. You and I both know that the septic system out there is not ready for a final clearance, and no one has called my office for a final."

Leaving the city official's office and puzzled by what he had just learned, Marshal next contacted the city's chief residential building official and asked if he could simultaneously interview every city inspector who had conducted inspections at the Bullock house while it was being built. The official agreed to Marshal's request. Marshal then contacted Dale Morgan, who had agreed to attend the meeting with the city inspectors and serve as a witness.

Dale had turned into a reliable witness. Just as he had promised, on the very day that Marshal had met with the trustees at the guesthouse, Dale had secured almost all of the plans and specifications and other construction documents that Marshal needed. His source had been one of the superintendents who had been fired by the builder but who maintained possession of the documents.

Dale had then carried about six large boxes of documents to the trustee's offices at the third floor of the Miller Building that was located on Sixth Street five blocks west of Marshal's office. Within another few days, Dale gathered even more documents, and the trustee and Marshal had begun combing through the documents. Over time, the Miller Building served as a resource center for the printing and dissemination of documents, and the entire third floor ultimately served as the command center for the trial of Sandra Bullock versus her builder.

Marshal and Dale met at Austin City Hall at the appointed time to meet with the city inspectors. They then walked into a conference room where a dozen city inspectors were sitting around a large conference table, waiting for them.

Marshal asked most of the questions. Some of the inspectors stated that they had seen so much poor-quality construction work going on that they felt powerless to stop it. Some said that they had begged their supervisors to send them to other projects so that they would not have to return to inspect the Bullock house. Finally, one of the department heads said that he had told the builder to hire a third-party independent inspector because the city inspectors would no longer conduct inspections of that particular project. Marshal told the inspectors that he had already talked with that particular inspector who had confirmed seeing numerous violations of the building codes. The inspector had also told Marshal that he issued correction notices to the builder's superintendents, but once he had returned to reinspect the project, the work had been covered up with other materials. He told Marshal that "they covered up a lot of stuff" and "I never cleared the framing."

Marshal told the city inspectors that he had observed cracking in the walls on the second floor above the entry area, which was a potential sign of the beginning of failure of the supporting floor trusses. One of the inspectors then said that he had seen a heavy fireplace sitting on the trusses at that location during construction and that it was his opinion that the builder had overloaded some of the trusses. He also said that he had seen some trusses in another part of the house that appeared to have been "chainsawed," meaning that it looked like someone had damaged the trusses by cutting a portion of them away in a jagged manner. He also said that the city issued an order to the builder that an engineer must certify that the trusses are safe and that the city had not received that certification.

As the meeting adjourned, Marshal thanked the inspectors for their willingness to help. He knew that city inspectors often catch the blame from the general public for what goes wrong on a construction project, when it is actually the contractor and not the inspector who is at fault. He also knew that many contractors play a game with the inspectors, leaving some construction items deliberately out of compliance so that the inspector can catch them, while other nonconforming items are covered up by the contractor hoping the inspector will miss them. Ultimately, it is next to impossible for the city inspectors to catch everything that can be wrong with construction projects. That's the job of the builder's superintendents.

As Dale and Marshal left City Hall, Dale said, "I've got another surprise for you. The builder has evidently been avoiding responsibility by shifting blame. He's blaming Sandra Bullock and the superintendents for all of the problems out there, but one of the superintendents told me that they were told by the builder what to do while building that house. That particular superintendent protected himself as the house was being built."

"Protected himself? How?" asked Marshal.

"He made videotapes of the construction progress while the work was going on. He evidently didn't tell the builder what he was doing."

"Can you get the videotapes?"

"I've got them right here in my briefcase," said Dale. "Here." as he handed the videotapes to Marshal.

Marshal returned to his office, opened the credenza that housed a TV and VHS player, and dropped the first video cassette into the player. The videotape revealed damaged wood floor trusses above the entry foyer with a subsequent repair with plywood reinforcer side plates that had been nailed to the trusses.

Wood floor trusses are a prefabricated structural component consisting of 2x4 wood members connected to each other with metal connector plates. The metal plates have small metal teeth that, when pressed into the joints where the wood members intersect, form a tight connection for the various members. The truss supplier fabricates the trusses in a plant, and the completed trusses are then shipped to the jobsite. Trusses are rarely, if ever, shipped to a site with plywood reinforcer plates already attached to them because the plywood reinforcer plates are installed in the field after a truss begins to break. Plywood reinforcers and peeling metal connector plates in installed trusses are usually signs of truss damage caused by overloading, fabrication, or design defects. Floor trusses, and any subsequent repairs, are supposed to be designed, reviewed, and certified by a professional engineer in order to assure the owner and the city that the trusses are safe for their intended use.

After reviewing the videotapes, Marshal then drove to the Bullock house, entered the large main foyer area, climbed on a tall stepladder that workers had been using, and removed some of the recessed light fixtures in the ceiling. He was able to inspect several second-floor trusses within the ceiling space from that particular vantage point. He saw that the plywood reinforcer plates had been improperly nailed to the trusses. He saw that plywood reinforcer plates had not been installed at some locations where some steel connector plates had partially withdrawn from the wood, indicating possible continuing joint failure in the trusses. *That would explain the cracking in the room above,* Marshal thought. *This floor system is failing. It's only a matter of time before it collapses completely.*

The city inspectors had insisted that an engineer certify that the trusses were safe. Marshal then drove back to the Miller Building to find a document that bore a certification from the wood truss supplier. He found a certification letter, but that particular document did not bear the seal of a professional engineer—just a signature.

Then Marshal compared the certification letter with some truss detail sheets that bore the seal of the engineer who had designed the trusses. The engineer had signed his name over his seal. When Marshal compared the signature on the sealed sheets with the signature on the certification letter, he saw that the name was the same on both documents, but the signatures did not even closely match. Even the type font that had been used to type the certification letter looked misaligned and did not match other text on the same document.

The truss certification document was an obvious forgery. With regard to the pending litigation, the investigation of the construction of Sandra Bullock's house was leading Marshal down a path of not only being a civil legal case; it was turning into a possible criminal case as well.

6

෨ MOTION TO STRIKE ෩

Bernie Rothenstein, Attorney at Law, strode into his large marble-and mahogany-lined office, leaving the door open wide behind him. Rothenstein was a tall, heavy man—a 'superlawyer.' He was in his mid-fifties and a powerful man in every sense of the word. He was followed by two lesser men, shorter in height and less bulky in girth.

Ignoring the two men, Rothenstein tossed his extra-large suit coat toward the sofa, loosened his tie, opened his sweat-stained collar, and flopped into the large custom-leather chair behind his desk. Beads of sweat glistened on top of his bald head then streaked down his meat-wrinkled face and over his thick lips. Patches of sweat stained the underarms of his white shirt.

Rothenstein spun his chair. He reached toward the five open boxes of tissues that sat on the credenza, grabbed a fistful, and mopped his brow and the top of his head.

It was the middle of summer 2004, the day before the trial of Sandra Bullock versus her builder was scheduled to begin.

"Ruth! When are they going to fix the blasted air conditioning on this floor?" he shouted in his thick, Bronx-native accent. "It's stifling hot in here. These windows face west, and it's still morning! I get a great view of the Texas Capitol, but otherwise they are useless! They can't even be opened!"

"I've called building management four times this morning, Mr. Rothenstein," Ruth yelled back from her secretarial desk on the other side of the open door. "They say they've fixed the eighteenth floor,

47

and our floor is the next one to be repaired. They say the air conditioning should be fully functional and working again on the nineteenth floor before noon."

Rothenstein reached into his desk drawer. He pulled out a Cuban cigar and lit it. He looked at the two engineers who were still standing. "Sit down, boys. Take a load off."

"Ruth!" he yelled again. "Come close the blasted door and turn on my cigar smoke filter from out there."

Joe Tuel, a professional engineer, sat down in front of the desk in the chair to Rothenstein's right. Dick Fuelem, another professional engineer, sat in the chair to Rothenstein's left. By the time they were seated, Ruth had shut the door and had gone back to her workstation.

Rothenstein stuck his cigar in the corner of his mouth. He stared at Dick Fuelem without saying a word. Fuelem was an engineer in his early thirties, slick black hair, short in stature, small chest and pear-shaped bottom, wearing a yellow pullover shirt and blue jeans. The horizontal, broad black patterns across Fuelem's yellow shirt made him look like a big bumblebee. Fuelem looked like some kind of bug as he craned his head and stared at the inlaid marble on the floor, the gold leaf inlays on the ceiling, and the two large Picassos on the wall. His wide girth below the belt had him wedged into the chair. Rothenstein started to snicker.

"Dick, you need to lose a little weight," Rothenstein said, trying not to laugh.

Fuelem looked at Rothenstein and remained quiet. *You could lose a few pounds yourself, Porky*, Fuelem thought to himself.

Rothenstein then looked at Joe Tuel. Tuel was Rothenstein's key man, an engineer in his early sixties who knew which side his bread was buttered on. The sparse gray hair on top of his head made Tuel's head look almost flat; and his broad cheeks covered by a full gray beard made his face look unnaturally wide. Parts of Tuel's beard were damp from sweat. In spite of the heat in the office, he still had his suit coat on. *Clowns*, Rothenstein thought to himself, *and these are my engineering expert witnesses.*

"Tuel," Rothenstein said calmly, "what in the world do you think you are doing, letting Fuelem here spill the beans to Marshal Yeager?"

"I'm sorry, Mr. Rothenstein," Fuelem said before Tuel could answer. "It won't happen again."

Rothenstein looked away from Tuel and glared at Fuelem. "What do you mean it won't happen again? Are you crazy? You've already said too much, Fuelem! Now we've got to figure out what to do about your stupidity! Do you have any idea how much money you might have lost for a lot of people? I'll tell you how much. It's billions of dollars!"

Rothenstein stopped talking as he puffed on his cigar. He was thinking as he stared beyond the two engineers at one of the Picassos on the far wall of his cavernous office. He had become aware of Marshal Yeager decades before and only recently he had heard the name spoken again. Rothenstein then looked back at Tuel. "Tell me, Tuel, what do you know about Marshal Yeager?"

"I know that Yeager can't be bought," Tuel said.

Rothenstein slammed his fist on top of his desk. "Everyone can be bought! You two sure were! What's his price?"

"I'm telling you, Mr. Rothenstein, Marshal Yeager cannot be bought," Tuel said. "He has been on my tail for the past five or six years, working for homeowners and testifying against my engineering opinions. Now that he's got Dick here to talk, he's not going to let it go. He's like a bulldog. I don't know what to do about him."

"What's his reputation?" Rothenstein inquired. "You've got friends at the Texas Board of Professional Engineers. What's his reputation down there?"

"They tell me that he has no disciplinary history at all," Tuel said. "He's clean."

"All right, you guys," said Rothenstein. "We're going to think this situation through, and you guys try to use your so-called scientific engineering methodology and maybe we can come up with a resolution to the problem. First, Fuelem, how did this whole situation with Yeager get started with you?"

Fuelem hesitated, staying silent.

"Tell me, blast you!" Rothenstein shouted.

"Well, Mr. Rothenstein," Fuelem stuttered, "I . . . I was in our office and had just walked into our kitchen to get some coffee, and

Marshal Yeager was just sitting there, drinking hot tea."

"In your San Antonio office, not in Tuel's Dallas office, right?" asked Rothenstein.

"That's right," Tuel interjected. "I have Fuelem here running the San Antonio office of Tuel Foundation Engineering. As you know, I head up the TFE office in Dallas and . . ."

"Tuel! Shut up! I'm taking to Fuelem!" Rothenstein yelled, glaring at Tuel. "He can speak for himself, can't he?"

"Mr. Rothenstein," said Fuelem, "Marshal Yeager strung me along. I had just poured a cup of coffee, and he asked me to sit down and join him. I didn't have anything else to do at that time, so I didn't see any harm in it. Marshal started to ask me some questions about my career, and I told him how happy I was working for Mr. Tuel here. Then he got me talking about the Wire Cable Tensioning Institute standards. You know, the WCTI stressed cable foundation method that we claim to use when we design house foundations, and it just slipped out. He asked me what we engineers at TFE think about the WCTI method, and I answered that we stopped believing years ago that the system works . . . that we've been beefing up our designs, adding extra concrete and steel to the foundations that we design for homebuilders."

Rothenstein sat quietly, then after a few seconds he said, "So you actually confessed to Marshal Yeager that the WCTI standards are defective?"

"I knew the moment I said it that it was a mistake, Mr. Rothenstein," said Fuelem.

"Fuelem," Rothenstein said quietly. "Let me explain something to you. The guy sitting next to you, Tuel here, testifies in court all the time for me and my major homebuilders that the standards are good. Doesn't it sound a little strange to you that your boss says the standards are good in court, and you admit to Marshal Yeager that the standards are bad and that TFE does not allow its engineers to use them in the office unless they add more concrete and steel? What do you think will happen if Marshal Yeager spreads the word to the lawyers who work on behalf of his homeowner-clients? Those lawyers will just subpoena and use both of you to cross each other up. It will be very clear to a jury that one of you is lying about those stupid standards."

"Mr. Rothenstein," Tuel interrupted, "those foundation design standards have been very useful for our clients who are the major homebuilders in this country in driving out their smaller competition. Don't forget that."

"I haven't forgotten that," said Rothenstein. "The problem is that now Marshal Yeager knows what your little engineering group has been doing. The only thing we have working for us right now is that he is too tied up with that Sandra Bullock case and that he doesn't have time to mess around with you two. So Fuelem, Tuel here told me a little about your tactic to resolve the problem by changing that official record at the Round Rock City Hall. What's that all about?"

"Well," said Fuelem, "GrandTex Pacific is our mutual client, and Barbara—one of your junior law associates—is working on the case. What happened was that GrandTex Pacific had hired Dan Drapere, P.E., to design the foundation for the house. Once the house was finished, Cathy Dickerson and her husband bought the house, and pretty soon the house started showing signs of falling apart mainly because the foundation was founded on expansive clay soils and was moving. I wrote a report for GrandTex Pacific in January of this year. There were a lot of problems with the cracked slab sitting in soaking wet clay and water seeping up through the floor. The second-floor wood trusses and the roof framing were also really in bad shape, sagging and cracking. Barbara told me that as an expert witness I could admit that there were problems with the superstructure frame, but she told me not to admit that there were problems with the foundation."

"That's right Fuelem, you never say anything is wrong with a WCTI-designed foundation, even if the expansive soils crack it all over the place and it seems like it is about to wrap around your head like a big rubber sheet because it is so flimsy," Rothenstein said.

"Then the Dickersons hired Marshal Yeager," continued Fuelem. "Marshal inspected the house a few weeks after I did. That was several months after Marshal tricked me into talking at my own office. It was Marshal Yeager who told Cathy Dickerson to go to City Hall to copy all of the city permit and inspection information she could find. She did what he told her to do. She found a certification form signed by Dan Drapere that indicated that the foundation had been designed for the type of soils that exhibited low-expansive qualities—in other words, minimal clay soil, mostly loam that will not cause foundations to move when exposed to a lot of water during rainstorms. It's just a general problem with building foundations on expansive clay soils here.

"I called Drapere, and he admitted to me that he had designed the foundation for another location about fifteen miles away from the Dickerson house. That location had low-expansion soils. He said that GrandTex Pacific had decided to also build the same plan at the subdivision that has the expansive clay soils which is where the Dickersons live. That is why the Dickersons' house is moving and cracking. It's the wrong foundation for those types of soils. Drapere's design was not intended to take the forces that are imposed on the underside of the foundation by the expanding clay soils. Drapere admitted to me that he made a mistake by not insisting that GrandTex Pacific furnish him with copies of all plans that they reuse for other locations. I simply wanted to get Drapere to issue another certification letter that said that he properly designed the foundation for the expansive clay soils at the Dickersons' house."

Rothenstein took the cigar out of his mouth and held it in his right hand. He looked down and placed the fingertips of his left hand to his damp forehead, and then he looked up at Fuelem.

"In other words, you propose taking an engineer's new certification letter, a false certification I might add, and exchanging that certification letter for the real one that exists in the City of Round Rock official files."

"It's only so that I can testify that the foundation design meets the WCTI standards," Fuelem protested. "I'm just making sure the certification fits what I need to say in my testimony. If I don't do it, our builder-client—GrandTex Pacific—will lose the lawsuit that the Dickersons brought."

"Fuelem," Rothenstein said, "do you have any legal counsel, any lawyer that might be advising you?"

"No, Mr. Rothenstein," Fuelem said. "I thought if any legal issues came up that you would represent me."

"No, Fuelem. I can't represent you. My associate, Barbara, is representing the builder in this case—GrandTex! You and Tuel are her expert witnesses. That's a conflict."

Rothenstein thought for a moment and then asked, "Did Drapere actually prepare a new certification letter?"

"He sure did," Fuelem said. "He's already had it delivered. This afternoon I'm going to Round Rock to switch Drapere's new certification letter for the original letter that's still there. Then Barbara can get me to testify in court that there is nothing wrong with the foundation because I can use the new certification to show that the foundation is okay and the homeowners will lose their lawsuit."

"There are at least two things wrong with your plan," said Rothenstein. "One, if you get caught making the switch, you and Tuel here are going to go to jail, and I can't afford to let that happen. It is illegal to alter a public record unless the engineer has a verifiable reason for doing so, and you don't have that reason other than to try to save GrandTex Pacific from a guaranteed loss as a result of this lawsuit that the Dickersons filed. Your second problem is that Marshal Yeager already has a copy of the original certification letter that his clients, the Dickersons, found months ago at City Hall. He can just pull that out of his file at the arbitration hearing and show the arbitrator what you did."

"How about if all of the files on the Dickerson house suddenly disappear from the city?" asked Fuelem. "That way I won't have to insert the new certification into the city files at all. Then all Marshal has is a copy, but I will have the original. Or I can just make a copy, have an official city seal made, stamp it as received by the city, copy that, and testify from that copy."

Oh, Lord, Rothenstein thought to himself. *I did so enjoy practicing law. Thanks to this Fuelem idiot the Texas, New York, and Washington DC Bar Associations will jerk all of my licenses to practice law at the same time. They might even send ME to jail.*

"So what you propose now," said Rothenstein, "is that you steal all the documents from the city file in order to eliminate the need to put the new document into the file. Then you could bring a copy of a new document that you stamped, with a stamp that you made, so that you could then testify that 'Here is the new certification from Drapere and it is the correct one. Foundation is okay. Homebuilder wins. Homebuyers lose. End of story.' Do I have that right?"

"Sounds reasonable to me," said Fuelem.

Rothenstein reached into his desk drawer for his heart medicine. He took a tablet out of a container and put it in his mouth. He began to chew slowly. He knew that he had to calm down.

"Boys, I'm a civil defense lawyer. I am thought by others to be a Republican, but really I'm just in it to make a lot of money so I go both ways, party-wise. I represent homebuilders and insurance companies, and they are the ones with all the money. The plaintiff lawyers are my opponents. They represent the homebuyers. They are mostly Democrats, but they make money, too.

"Do you boys know how much poverty in our cities is caused by Democrat progressive policies? I'll give you some examples. Miami and El Paso have never had Republican mayors, and 26% of the populace in both cities is below the poverty level. Newark hasn't elected a Republican mayor since 1907, and 24% of the people are poor. Milwaukee—no Republican mayor since 1908, and 26% of those people are poor. St. Louis, not a one since 1949, almost 27% poor. Philadelphia . . . since 1952—25% poor. Buffalo hasn't elected one since 1954, and downtown is almost deserted; of those who remain in the city, almost 30% are poor. And the granddaddy of them all . . . the poorest city in the nation is Detroit, which hasn't elected a Republican mayor since 1961, and almost 33% of the populace is made up of poor Blacks, Mexicans, and Muslims. It is the poor who keep electing Democrats, and of course they stay poor. That's what happens when the Democrats tax business to death and also the rest of the people, in order to keep them enslaved. Problem is, the Republicans can't quite reverse the trend because most of them really don't want to.

"'You cannot help the poor by destroying the rich. You cannot strengthen the weak by weakening the strong. You cannot bring about prosperity by discouraging thrift. You cannot lift the wage earner up by pulling the wage payer down. You cannot further the brotherhood of man by inciting class hatred. You cannot build character and courage by taking away people's initiative and independence. You cannot help people permanently by doing for them what they could and should do for themselves.' Do you boys know who said that?"

The two engineers stared at Rothenstein blankly. Then Tuel said, "Abraham Lincoln?"

"Bzzzzaaap, wrong," said Rothenstein. "Those lines are often attributed to Lincoln, but the lines were written and published in 1916 by a Presbyterian minister named William J. H. Boetcker in a pamphlet titled *The Ten Cannots* and, as reprinted by a conservative group in 1942, they were included within a pamphlet titled *Lincoln on Limitations*. The original pamphlet did include a quote by Lincoln, but Boetcker was the one who added the statements. You boys need to get your noses out of those engineering journals and read some good books sometime. That's what we lawyers do—we read books. That's how we control people like you, and look where we are today. We control Congress, the presidency, labor unions, management, the courts, the news media, the school systems, the banking system, the FDIC, the SEC, the Federal Reserve, everything."

Tuel was growing upset at Rothenstein's remarks. "Mr. Rothenstein, even though you and I work together, I can tell you that I have met some lawyers who do not think the same way that you do, and I resent you telling us that you control people like us."

"Those lawyers are losers!" Rothenstein said. "I win, and they don't. That's why my minimum fee is $1500 per hour. I'm telling you where a lot of lobbyists and political lawyers like me come from. I'm not speaking for the entire legal profession or even about your engineering profession. During electoral campaigns every four years, we've got members of both political parties begging for money, and if they agree to do what we tell them, then we pay the ones we want, whether they are Republicans or Democrats. Then they pretend to fight each other with whiny meaningless but important-sounding sound bites like 'I'm for abortion' versus 'I'm against abortion'; 'I'm for the environment' versus 'I'm for private property'; 'I'm for minorities getting taxpayer money' versus 'I'm for individual initiative and free enterprise and low taxes.' The same stupid sound bites have been repeated every four years in political campaigns for generations.

"Then for those incumbents who survive the elections, and over ninety-five percent of them do survive, we all get together, Republicans and Democrats alike, and we have a big party and make tons of money for the next three years. Then we start the process all over again. They get a guaranteed high-dollar pension plan and medical plan for serving even one term in Congress, and we get lots of earmarks that we can spread around. We are the ones behind the politicians; we are the invisible true captains of industry and labor. Do you really think the American people are ever going to wake up and see what's happening to them? Of course not, as long as we control both the banking system and the news media through the Federal Reserve. Although I do admit I am a little concerned about the Internet, but eventually we'll find a way to control that through regulation.

"Do you boys have any real reason to believe that NAFTA was passed to benefit this nation? I sure don't have any real reason to believe it, but it certainly does benefit people like me. I'm a mover and shaker, and NAFTA and the Environmental Protection Agency are two of the most ingenious plans for some of us to make massive amounts of money that ever came down the pike. Industry and jobs leave the nation as a result of the EPA mandates, and I make money through my foreign partners. With the NAFTA treaty, the Federal Reserve can work internationally to provide the financial vehicle that gets Americans borrowing money and buying things that they don't need, generating the taxes that keep us in power. Then they find themselves working off the high debt load that they incurred in order to attend college, while sitting in all their little work cubicles trying to pay for all of it, when all they really wanted to do in life was farm, raise a family, play music, or work with their hands in a trade. Why do you think we did what we could to abolish vocational training schools? Fools! We used the FDIC to steal as many farms and ranches as we could get in the 1980s, and now the farmers are our tenants. The nation needs cheap, controllable worker bees housed in some big corporation, not individuals running their own businesses and competing with the big boys. Nobody gets rich in America anymore unless we let them, and if they succeed without us, then we find out

56

how they do it through our contacts within the banking system, and then we use the government to destroy them by using the monetary system.

"Around 1980, the financial services industry comprised about two percent of the gross domestic product. Now it comprises more than six percent. And name me something tangible that the financial services industry has produced over the last three decades, other than the ATM machine. Even that machine was invented by engineers and not by bankers. Most Americans are now so enslaved to the world and so deep in debt that they may never claw their way out. Do you think that it was just an accident?"

Rothenstein turned around in his chair and faced the books on the shelves behind him. He stood up and searched until he found the one. "Here, Tuel, take this book home and read it," as he tossed the book to Tuel. "It's an advance edition of *Deception and Abuse at the Fed: Henry B. Gonzalez Battles Alan Greenspan's Bank* by Robert D. Auerbach. Read about how the Federal Reserve took over the U.S. Treasury during the days of Harry Truman, and read about all the money that the Fed siphoned off to loan to other countries beginning in the late 1970s through insider trading 'swaps' without most members of Congress or the taxpayer knowing anything about it. All along we've had just enough people in Congress to hold off auditing the Fed, while the Fed drains the taxpayers dry and loans the money indirectly to foreign businesses and American businesses that move overseas. You're now a big part of this racket, boys, and I want both of you to know where your money is really coming from."

Rothenstein sat down again. "I'll tell you a little story, boys. We got that George W. Bush in a squeeze out in Midland in 1983, long before he became president of the United States. We worked with both the FDIC and the Federal Reserve to nail his behind to the wall in a collapsed banking deal while his daddy was vice president. Paul Volcker, who headed the Federal Reserve back then, met privately with President Reagan and then, what do you know, Reagan reappointed Volcker to the Federal Reserve right at the beginning of the Texas Depression. That was about the time Reagan was starting to worry about being reelected, and he couldn't tolerate the son of his vice president being in trouble.

"Do you boys know what a 'government–corporation partnership' really is? You hear a little about it, like a city going into partnership with a sports franchise to build a football stadium, or a corporation getting a city to exercise eminent domain condemnation of private property in order to enhance economic development. But what we did with the FDIC was absolutely beautiful. We had the FDIC stealing private property and actually giving it to us.

"It took a few of my El Paso associates who contracted with the FDIC to do their legal work, but we got the mission accomplished and were able to acquire billions of dollars in oil royalties and surface assets through our use of the FDIC and our manipulation of the court system. We had to arrange for a few personal mishaps along the way, but 'W' never knew what had happened around him until after he became president. Even now, he has that blank look while the whole country wonders who is really at the helm of the presidency. I suspect the Federal Reserve will keep manipulating him until about the end of his term and then they will collapse the economy the same way they collapsed the economy in Texas and much of the rest of the nation in the 1980s. That's why the next few years are going to be very critical for my homebuilder-clients and why they need to begin to finish development of their new subdivisions and start draining their money and putting it overseas.

"Now here in Texas under Governor Rick Perry, we have a new form of the modern-day government–corporation partnership between the new Texas Residential Construction Commission and my homebuilding corporations. That commission is going to be my delaying mechanism to keep the homebuyers at bay while my builders finish their projects and then move elsewhere.

"And pretty soon, I will have the Texas Board of Professional Engineers eating out of my hands and protecting my homebuilders from engineers like Marshal Yeager. My people at the staff level have been in place for the past few weeks and have already nailed one Dallas engineer who has been testifying against homebuilders and insurance corporations. Pretty soon I'll have others on the staff that will do what I want them to do. I've also chased off the Board's executive director over that Bonfire collapse incident. She never should have mentioned to the media that the Board intended to investigate the Texas A&M engineering faculty about their ethical duty, but I've put a stop to that investigation, and now she's gone. There's one engineering professor there that I definitely do not want involved in any kind of investigation because he knows all about our scam with the WCTI foundation standards. In case you boys haven't heard, the City of San Antonio Housing Authority has said 'no más,' or 'no more' to those standards. Pretty soon other cities in Texas will probably ban those standards, so we've only got a few more years to slap a bunch of those foundations on the clay soil, finish our houses, and move on out.

"Boys, a small number of people like me are running the whole world on an international level through the Federal Reserve while most Americans are worked and taxed, cradle to grave, and distracted by fake political issues, entertainment, and worrying about their jobs. But my eye is now on state government, and Texas is where I am focusing my attention.

"Now why am I telling you boys all of this? It's because I need you to help me, and if you do, you will have more wealth than you can possibly ever imagine."

"Dick Fuelem and I?" said Tuel. "How can we help?"

"Keep up what you have been doing," said Rothenstein. "In court cases, never provide engineering calculations that can be rebutted, so destroy your calculations before the other side can get hold of them. Lie like crazy in court but skillfully enough to fool the judge or arbitrator, and just be consistent in what you say about those WCTI foundation standards."

Rothenstein paused, thinking. "Here's something that you engineers should be able to grasp. Tuel, do you remember the 1970s-era Ford Pinto that would explode when struck from behind?"

"I sure do," Tuel said. "I knew someone who died when his Pinto was in a rear-end collision. It exploded just like you said."

"I've been practicing law for many decades," Rothenstein said, "and with globalism and the buying of American industries by foreign investors, I have become very excited by what appears to be a resurgence of the old Ford business model, particularly in the homebuilding industry. We have now entered a new era of what is disparagingly termed 'greed and corruption' and that I term 'vast wealth and opportunity.' The corporate culture of various industries in the United States is becoming compromised by an increasing demand for profits that results in a corresponding reduction in consideration for the public health, safety, and welfare—something you engineers are supposed to know about. At Ford back then, it seemed like the culture tended to compromise the moral principles of those professional engineers whose livelihoods depended on an industry for employment, while their licenses to practice depended on their assurances to the public that their designs were safe.

"What happened was that in the early 1970s, Ford Motor Company's engineers designed a fuel system in the Ford Pinto that was defectively placed. The fuel system resulted in many deaths and injuries when the cars were struck from behind at a relatively low rate of speed and the gas tanks exploded. Ford had utilized a cost-benefit analysis and decided not to upgrade the fuel system based on that particular analysis. Although Ford had access to a new design that would decrease the possibility of the Pinto exploding, the company chose not to implement the design for reasons related to cost. It would have cost $11 per car even though the analysis showed that the new design would result in 180 fewer deaths.

"Of course, Ford has worked hard to reverse that image. However, what really excites me now is that Ford's corporate business model of that era has been taught to other large industries, and over time it has been extended into the homebuilding industry. The large-scale interstate homebuilding industry has learned and accepted, just like Ford learned and has subsequently rejected, that the cost of defending lawsuits is lower than the cost of making expensive redesigns or correcting construction defects. That is why the homebuilders would rather go to court or arbitration than make repairs. The big money is in using the cheapest foundations they can and never fixing them.

"With the passage of time," Rothenstein continued, "I have observed the gradual evolution and escalation of disputes between Texas homebuyers and homebuilders. Practicing law, I have consistently asked homebuilders and their insurance companies to find engineering experts like you two who will tell a judge or arbitrator that either nothing is wrong with a buyer's house, or if something is obviously wrong, agreeing to give the homebuyer a small amount of money to patch the cracks.

"It's the willingness of you two engineers, Tuel and Fuelem, to compromise your ethics and go to court and defend the homebuilder's product against the homebuyers. When you do that, we can pay both of you vast sums of money based simply on your engineering opinions. The homebuilders, who I represent, can still make a huge profit building homes with flimsy foundations and also defending lawsuits, as compared to the smaller profit we would make if homebuilders used better and more-expensive foundation systems.

"Tuel, your biggest challenge for several years now, has been to deflect the opinions of opposing engineers who work for homebuyers and who find structural defects. Those engineers have consistently stated that structural problems in houses often relate to design or construction of the home's foundation system, and they testify to me that approximately ninety percent of the concrete slab-on-ground foundations that are founded on expansive clay soils, and that exhibit excessive flexing or other movement characteristics, are the tensioned steel cable concrete foundation systems—the same types of foundations that your engineers are designing to standards but also beefing up, not to perfection which would increase our costs, but just close enough to give us time to get out before cracking and foundation movement begins.

"What is now really making it easy for all of us is that I have been working with some other lawyers involved in defending homebuilders, and several years ago we came up with standard sales contract language our builders can use that calls for binding arbitration, which keeps everything out of court. And now, thanks to Governor Perry, we have tort reform, which brought about the Texas Residential Construction Commission—the agency I mentioned that provides a roadblock and that protects my homebuilders from the homebuying consumer.

"But wouldn't you think that now we have the best of all possible worlds? Not yet. It gets even better. I'm getting both of your backsides protected at the Texas Board of Professional Engineers. In a few weeks you boys will be bulletproof. Governor Perry has appointed some people to that Board who are favorable to me.

"You boys probably know that the only real power the governor of Texas has is the power to appoint members to boards and commissions and the power to veto legislation. In the 2001 legislative session, Rick Perry vetoed many bills, apparently to warn the legislators that if they didn't send him bills that reflected his wishes and the wishes of his financial contributors, he would veto everything. The Legislature meets every other year, so in 2003, some real headway was made by the corporations that I represent, especially the major homebuilders, because Rick Perry did not veto our bills. In fact, his major contributors were the homebuilders who pushed the bills through the Texas Legislature.

"Also, the plan has been in the works for some time now to carve up Texas into wide strips through eminent domain laws, with toll roads built by a foreign company, and to begin construction of the NAFTA superhighway starting at the border between Texas and Mexico. They are even talking about importing thousands of technicians from the Middle and Far East through Mexico, Canada, and Australia, who will work like cheap monkeys on their computers and be under our control once those countries call them real engineers and get it past the Texas Board of Professional Engineers. Then they go nationwide through the National Council of Engineering Examiners and Surveyors, which sets uniform standards of examination, licensing, and conduct. Every professional engineer in the nation will eventually be under our control through the power of the state engineering boards to discipline engineers and even take away their licenses if they get too politically involved against us. We're going to have cheap, international so-called engineers designing the NAFTA superhighway. There's talk now of the state's voters keeping Perry from building his toll roads, but even if the project is temporarily scaled back, we have people in the Texas Legislature who will put it back into place for us in the future.

"I'll tell you boys why Texas is so important to us. Texas is the most lucrative market in the United States for homebuilding. It's easy to get started here, and it's a $35 billion industry. The state's business-friendly political climate is practically devoid of regulatory accountability. There are no homebuilder licensing, capital, or insurance requirements. Rick Perry's tort reform laws provide protection from lawsuits, imported Mexican labor is plentiful, and land is inexpensive. Down-payment assistance programs help renters buy homes. The volume builders have their own mortgage companies, subsidized loans, and inflated appraisals. And you engineers are able to grind out cheap foundations here.

"We've tried for decades to change the United States Constitution by getting our international advocates appointed to the U.S. Supreme Court, with some limited success, but it's taking way too long. Justice Anthony Kennedy wrote in *Lawrence v. Texas* that 'the right to homosexual sodomy has been accepted in many other countries,' so he's one of ours who is willing to help us use foreign courts to change U.S. laws. Another is Justice John Paul Stevens who wrote in *Atkins v. Virginia* that 'within the world community, the imposition of the death penalty for crimes committed by mentally retarded offenders is overwhelmingly disapproved.' And Justices Ruth Bader Ginsburg and Stephen Breyer concurred in *Grutter v. Bollinger* to justify the University of Michigan Law School's racial preference program by citing a United Nations treaty.

"Imposing international law on the United States at the Supreme Court level is just not getting us where we want to be fast enough. But if we take over the practice of engineering in America, then we can control what's left of the nation's industrial strength and soon after that the capabilities of the United States military. Texas is our highway to globalism and internationalism, and the road to international law replacing constitutional law in this nation is going to come right up through Mexico into the United States along the NAFTA superhighway. Tuel, your professor buddy at Texas A&M has never been able to convince the majority of his engineering peers that the WCTI method works, so we have disbanded all of the major building-code agencies in this country and combined that authority into a unified code authority operating as the International Building Code and International Residential Code. Those codes are now the law of the land for building and housing construction in the United States, and they cannot be violated. And what that means is that engineers must follow the international law as a minimum standard no matter what! And what is 'international law?' It's not U.S. Constitutional law, you can be darn sure of that. It's going to be Sharia law—Islamic law. It takes trillions of petrodollars to finance a takeover like this, and a large chunk of that money flows to me.

"Notice I said 'minimum standard.' Engineers are empowered to exceed the standard in their designs, but we're also getting rid of that power. We're also going to get rid of 'engineering judgment.' We're going to force the engineers to design their foundations to the WCTI standards, even though all of us in this room know the standards don't work. And how are we going to do that? Now that we've got the WCTI standards contained within the International Residential Code, we're going to eliminate the other engineering design options contained in that code. And for those engineers who try to exceed the standards, the state engineering boards are going to discipline them and take away their licenses for being environmentally wasteful. We are going to apply the environmentalist position that engineers call for too many materials to be put in structures, and that results in waste and expenditure of too much energy. Governor Perry appointed the members to the Texas Board of Professional Engineers—the Board controls the staff—and the staff is tweaking the rules just enough so that no one will know what's going on until it's too late."

Rothenstein reached for a sheet of paper on his desk and handed it to Tuel. "Here, Tuel, read this out loud for Fuelem."

Tuel began to read:

> Section 137.55, Engineers Shall Protect the Public—
> Engineers shall not perform any engineering function which, when measured by generally accepted engineering standards or procedures, is reasonably likely to result in endangerment of lives, health, safety, property, or welfare of the public. Engineers should strive to adequately examine the environmental impact of their actions and projects, including the prudent use and conservation of resources and energy, in order to make informed recommendations and decisions.

"'Generally accepted engineering standards,'" interrupted Rothenstein. "Those are your WCTI standards, and soon no others will be allowed for designing house foundations. Also you must be 'prudent' in the use of materials and no excess materials can be used. Okay, Tuel, continue reading."

Tuel continued:

> Section 131.15(a)(3), Compliance and Enforcement Committee—The committee shall meet to develop proposed actions for the full board on enforcement issues, and for suggesting sanctions for violations of the Act; furthermore, the committee shall meet to participate in national and international engineering law enforcement activities on the board's behalf.

"Boys," said Rothenstein, "the first provision has just now been adopted by the Texas Board of Professional Engineers through the Board's rulemaking authority, and the second one is on the way to adoption. What those provisions mean is that any engineer who does not do exactly what the International Building Code says, and no more, will get his license jerked by the enforcement committee of any state board that adopts those provisions. And international law does not include rights for Americans under U.S. Constitutional law. You boys are about to witness your engineering competitors falling under my control through international law and my control of the state engineering boards. We couldn't have done any of this without Governor Rick Perry's cooperation. That's why we put him in power, and that's why we will keep him in that position at all costs until we make him president of the United States.

"I mentioned NAFTA a few minutes ago. Thanks to you, Tuel, millions of pounds of foreign steel cables are being manufactured at slave wages overseas, then shipped to this country and put into the foundation systems that you guys design. Do you really give a flip that thousands of American steel workers that make conventional reinforcing steel are put out of work because of what you are doing? I don't think so. You're doing so much better than those engineers in Austin and Fort Worth. I have steered to TFE, what . . . 300,000 steel cable concrete house foundations over the past several years? And what is your billing to design each foundation? Say, $1,000 per foundation? And then your net profit after you pay your employees is what, $100 per foundation? So by my calculation over the past five or so years you have made 30 million dollars before taxes, grinding out those foundations on your fancy computers for my major homebuilders that are making my steel cable companies in Korea and other countries quite rich."

Rothenstein turned to Fuelem now. "Of course we have Mr. Fuelem here who can't keep his big mouth shut to Marshal Yeager and who says that the foundation system you guys promote doesn't really work."

The speakerphone on Rothenstein's desk buzzed. "Mr. Rothenstein, I have what looks like the fax you were waiting for," the voice said.

"Bring it in here, Ruth," Rothenstein said.

The door opened, and Ruth walked in. She handed the fax to Rothenstein and then left the room, saying, "In case you didn't notice, the air conditioning is fixed." She closed the door behind her.

Rothenstein studied the faxed cover page and then the attached letter. He then said, "Boys, it looks like the judge is going to let Marshal Yeager testify in that trial that Sandra Bullock brought against Ezekiel Sheppaerd, the builder who constructed her house so poorly. This Response Motion to the builder's Motion to Strike Mr. Yeager from the case looks well drafted."

Handing the document to Tuel, Rothenstein said, "Give a copy of this to every homebuilder's lawyer that you work for, just in case the other side tries to get you disqualified from testifying. They can use it as a template."

Tuel looked at the document. It read:

> It is within this Court's discretion whether or not to admit Yeager's expert testimony. *Gammill v. Jack Williams Chevrolet, Inc.*, 972 S.W.2d 713, 727 (Tex.

1998). The Court's function, as the "gatekeeper," is not to determine if Yeager's conclusions are correct, but only whether his conclusions are relevant and whether his analysis in reaching his conclusions is reliable. *Id.* at 728. Upon review of Yeager's analysis and conclusions, this Court should deny Movants' Motion to Strike because Yeager's conclusions are reliable.

"Mr. Rothenstein, what is a 'Movants' Motion to Strike'?" asked Tuel.

"In this case," answered Rothenstein, "the 'Movants' are the homebuilder and subcontractors who are opposed to Sandra Bullock. The 'Motion to Strike' is a request by their lawyers to remove Marshal Yeager's report conclusions from the trial, meaning that he wouldn't even be able to testify at trial. Without him being able to testify to his conclusions, then Sandra Bullock will automatically lose her case even before the trial begins. Sandra Bullock's lawyers have filed this 'Response Motion' in an effort to prevent the judge from dismissing Marshal Yeager. Keep reading."

Tuel continued to read:

> Movants mischaracterize Yeager's testimony, conclusions, and opinions. They argue that Yeager improperly bases his findings of systemic deficiencies solely on single discovered deficiencies. The disputed deficiencies concern the second-floor and ceiling trusses.
>
> But, Movants do not dispute Yeager's expert qualifications—that he has extensive experience in residential construction—or his extensive observations of the residence—that he has personally documented and observed widespread deficiencies throughout the residence in virtually every observed area.
>
> Movants additionally mischaracterize the applicable law by stating that the Court "must inquire"

into certain factors to determine the admissibility of Yeager's testimony.

The United States and Texas Supreme Courts, however, have found that the "test of reliability is 'flexible'" and the "list of specific factors neither necessarily nor exclusively applies to all experts or in every case." *Kuhmo Tire Co., Inc., v. Carmichael,* 526 U.S. 137, 141–142, 119 S.Ct. 1167, 143 L.Ed. 2d 238, 246 (1999); *see also, Gammill,* 972. S.W.2d at 726 (The *Robinson* factors "for assessing the reliability of scientific evidence cannot always be used with other kinds of expert testimony."). "Rather, the law grants a district court the same broad latitude when it decides *how* to determine reliability as it enjoys with respect to its ultimate reliability determination." *Id.*

The Texas Supreme Court, for example, has noted that in some cases the expert's experience alone may be enough to show reliability. *Gammill,* 972 S.W.2d at 726. ("Experience alone may provide a sufficient basis for an expert's testimony in some cases . . .") In this case, Yeager's vast experience in residential construction similarly should support a reliability finding as to his opinions and conclusions on the disputed areas of testimony without further analysis. But, in addition to Yeager's experience, Yeager's conclusions have been tested, his conclusions have not been disproven, and his techniques are generally accepted as valid to determine deficiencies in residential construction. *See* Yeager Affidavit, pp. 2–3, ¶ 6.

There simply is no "analytical gap" between the data that Yeager relies upon and the opinions that he offers. *Gammill,* 972 S.W.2d at 726. Yeager comprehensively inspected the entire residence and observed and documented its vast deficiencies. The fact that he has not tested each and every truss for example may be a point for cross-examination, but it should not prevent his testimony and conclusions. *Id* at 728. ("The trial court's gatekeeping function under Rule 702 does not supplant cross-examination . . ."); *see also, Doyle Wilson Homebuilder, Inc., v. Pickens*, 996 S.W.2d 387 (Tex. App.—Austin 1999, pet. dism'd agr.). (Court properly allowed expert testimony and opinions that two unrelated defects in other part of house supported that same type of defect caused fire.)

Yeager's opinions and conclusions also are supported by other evidence, including other expert testimony and observations, further supporting a court finding of reliability and admissibility.

As to the truss issue, Yeager's conclusions in his report that the trusses require further inspection are supported by: (1) actual observation of visible trusses in entry area; (2) observation of other trusses through videotape; (3) conversations with City of Austin inspectors that confirmed that the contractor had overloaded some of the trusses and that inspector observed trusses that looked to have been "chainsawed"; (4) the fact that city requirement that an engineer certify the trusses as safe has not been met to date; (5) observed cracking in the floor on second story; and (6) the repair to the entry truss was improper and paperwork concerning the repair was forged. See Yeager Report, Exhibit A to Yeager Affidavit, filed contemporaneously herewith. This evidence coupled with Yeager's experience with trusses more than supports a finding of reliability as to Yeager's conclusions raising a question as to adequacy of the trusses, generally.

Movants also argue that the disputed areas of Yeager's testimony should be stricken because such testimony is within the general knowledge and experience of an average juror. In support of this argument, they cite a case that concerns the admissibility of expert testimony in an intentional infliction of emotional distress case. *GTE Southwest, Inc., v. Bruce*, 998 S.W.2d 605 (1999). In that case, at the trial, the experts testified that certain conduct was "extreme and outrageous." On appeal, the Supreme Court held that whether conduct is "extreme and outrageous" is an issue that was within general knowledge and experience so that expert testimony was not proper. *Id* at 619–620.

In contrast, Yeager is testifying about technical issues in a specialized area, residential construction, a subject that clearly is not within the common knowledge and experience of an average juror. Based on his knowledge and experience, his observations and conclusions will assist the jury in understanding the evidence and therefore are admissible. *See* Texas Rule of Evidence 702.

The cases that the Movants' cited in their Motion to Strike do not support striking Yeager's testimony. For example, Yeager's conclusions are not based on assumptions that have been conclusively disproved. *See Rayon v. Energy Specialties, Inc.*, 121 S.W.3d 7, 20 (Tex. App.—Ft. Worth 2002, no pet.). (Expert testimony held to be no evidence in summary judgment proceeding because testimony based on assumptions that conclusively disproved.)

In addition, Yeager's conclusions could have been readily controverted. *Id.* at 21. (Court looks to see if testimony could be "readily controverted" to determine if admissible.) All the actual evidence rather confirms that the defects in the residence are systemic. *See* Yeager report, February 26, 2001, at 10–11.

Further, Yeager's conclusions are not based on some hypothetical residence, but on actual observations of the actual residence. *See Guadalupe-*

Blanco River Authority v. Kraft, 77 S.W.3d 805, 810 (Tex. 2002). (Court disallowed expert appraisal testimony in condemnation proceeding that used "hypothetical tract reconfigured and relocated.")

Yeager's conclusions are far from based on "speculation on speculation" or "inference on inference." *See Marathon Corporation v. Pitzner*, 106 S.W.3d 724, 729 (Tex. 2003). (The Court disallowed expert testimony because known circumstances could have given "'rise to any number of inferences, none more probable then another.'") (citation omitted). Rather, Yeager's opinions are supported by the data and should be allowed at the trial to assist the trier of fact.

"Finished reading, Tuel?" Rothenstein said. "Did you see the word 'forged' in there?"

"I see it now," answered Tuel. "It's item six that says 'the repair to the entry truss was improper and paperwork concerning the repair was forged.' What's that all about?"

"It means," Rothenstein said, "that Marshal Yeager was observant enough to spot a forgery that could affect the entire case against Sandra Bullock's homebuilder. I've spoken with the builder's lawyer, and he is certain that the builder had nothing to do with the crime. He says it looks like the work of one of the suppliers of truss materials to the house, of which there were several such suppliers who were involved with their own truss engineers. However, as far as commitments between the builder and Sandra Bullock and her trustees were concerned, the builder was responsible to Sandra for the actions of the subcontractors and suppliers, and the builder's defense case could fall apart if Marshal Yeager was allowed to testify to the forgery that he discovered. That trial is supposed to be a civil trial involving a homebuyer and homebuilder, not a criminal one with an unknown defendant who committed a forgery and with no time left before the trial to try to find out who the author of the forgery might be.

"In an effort to prevent Marshal from testifying at trial, one of the builder's lawyers filed with the court a Motion to Strike the expert witness testimony of Marshal Yeager. Sandra Bullock's lawyers then filed the Response Motion you have in your hand. The judge heard the motion and agreed to allow Marshal Yeager to testify, although he won't be allowed to testify about the forgery. He's scheduled to testify in about three weeks. The trial starts tomorrow. One of the lawyers in this firm is representing one of the subcontractors."

"So how does that affect us?" asked Tuel.

"It means that Marshal Yeager is detail oriented," said Rothenstein. "Regarding our homebuilder-client, GrandTex Pacific who is being sued by the Dickersons, don't forget that Yeager already has a copy of the correct certification, and Mr. Fuelem here is proposing that he steal the Dickerson house records at City Hall."

Turning toward Fuelem, Rothenstein said, "Fuelem, you need to help us get Marshal Yeager once and for all. Are you willing to go all the way?"

"Whatever you say Mr. Rothenstein."

"Are you willing to assault his client, Cathy Dickerson?"

"What?" said Fuelem incredulously.

"Just verbally. Aggressive enough to get Yeager to file a complaint against you with the Texas Board of Professional Engineers," Rothenstein said.

"I don't know, Mr. Rothenstein. I'm not willing to risk my professional engineer's license."

"What about if you just pick a verbal confrontation with Yeager during a meeting. He could assert in a complaint that you lack professionalism. Why not try that first, just to get him to file a complaint?"

"I'll try that first, but if I lose my license, I want a lot of money for this," Fuelem said.

"I'll tell you what, Fuelem," said Rothenstein. "It is worth a lot of money to us to get rid of Marshal Yeager any way we can. He is far too honest and effective at working for homebuyers countering what Tuel here testifies to on behalf of homebuilders. Another problem is that this case of Sandra Bullock and her builder that he's working on is going to draw worldwide attention to the Texas homebuilding industry. It might expose what we have been trying to conceal from the FBI—the massive building and mortgaging Ponzi scheme we have going on down here. We have insiders at the SEC, but no one to help us at the FBI. We have the major interstate homebuilders using their integrated mortgage companies to loan money to people who can barely breathe, much less pay the money back, and then pawning off those loans onto secondary-market investors as mortgage-backed securities. Then those securities are insured with credit default swaps that are handled by New York Wall Street investors who, in turn, are slicing and dicing the mortgages into bundles, and then selling those bundles to foreign and domestic investors. The Chinese government is also buying our debt, and up until now they haven't had the faintest idea what is going on here. What worries me about the Sandra Bullock case is that I have heard a Chinese government representative will be there observing the proceedings, so they might be starting to catch on."

"How much money for me? I'm still not comfortable with this," said Fuelem.

"Don't worry," said Rothenstein. "I can guarantee that you will not be censured by the engineering Board. By the time we need you to do your little deed, we will have the right people in position. If we accidentally trip up and the engineering Board does revoke your license, I will place one million dollars in an overseas bank account for you."

"What about the certification that I got from Drapere . . . and what about the city records? What should I do about them? Should I make the switch?"

"Don't worry about that, Fuelem. I'm going to personally take over this case. Just have the original copy of the latest certification from Drapere with you when you arrive at the arbitration hearing, but I will still need to meet with you before that time. The records at the city are as good as gone. I just want you to personally stay away from City Hall."

"One million if I testify with the new Drapere certification letter, and *five* million if I lose my license," Fuelem countered.

The fire in Rothenstein's cigar had gone out. He grabbed his lighter and lit his cigar again. As the smoke curled toward the ceiling, Rothenstein stared into Fuelem's eyes and smiled. Fuelem was indeed the kind of greedy engineer he needed.

"Agreed," Rothenstein said.

7

CB THE TRIAL OF THE MOVIE STAR

VERSUS THE BUILDER BO

O n the morning of September 2, 2004, Marshal Yeager entered the Travis County courthouse in downtown Austin. He wore a gray business suit, white shirt, tie, and well-polished dress shoes. With his briefcase stuffed with documents and wearing his wire rim glasses, Marshal knew wearing a black or dark blue business suit could confuse others that he might be a lawyer; and even worse, a possible perception by the jury that he was really a lawyer in disguise who was pretending to be an engineer.

He passed through the security checkpoint at the courthouse door, took the elevator to the fifth floor, showed his identification to a court official who was guarding the courtroom door, and then entered the courtroom. He walked directly toward the judge's bench, past a large group of spectators and news reporters seated at the rear of the courtroom. There were no photographers; the judge had already banned cameras and cell phones from the courtroom.

The judge administered the oath to Marshal. "Do you solemnly swear that the testimony you are about to give is the truth, the whole truth, and nothing but the truth, so help you God?"

Marshal's sharp eyes focused on the judge. "I do."

"Please be seated," said the judge.

As Marshal stepped into the witness box, he first glanced at the jury, and then he tried to find where he could put his documents. The wooden ledge in front of the witness chair was too small for all of his papers, so he placed the materials he had brought with him on the floor next to the chair. Marshal then took his seat.

He looked around the small courtroom that had grown almost totally quiet. The defense table was toward his right, jammed directly against the wall. An easel holding an exhibit had been placed in front of the defense table and partially blocked his view in that direction. To his immediate right sat the judge, who by that time was speaking quietly to the lawyers who had approached the bench. To his left sat twelve jurors and a few alternates.

The plaintiff's table was located directly in front of him about fifteen feet away. Seated behind the table was Sandra Bullock, and to the left of her sat her father. The trial had already been underway for over two weeks before Marshal had been permitted to testify. Both Sandra and her father looked exhausted from the strain, but she was smiling at Marshal. The lawyers had begun the trial by presenting their opening arguments. Sandra's lawyer had described how her dream home had become a nightmare of broken promises, broken dreams, and failure to take responsibility, and she alleged that the builder had "committed fraud through questionable billing practices." The builder's lawyer countered that Sandra had made "significant changes in the design," the case was about a "broken relationship," and the jury must be impartial to an "Iranian builder with an accent."

When Sandra had testified, she acknowledged that she did not question the bills for months. She had testified that "nineteen months into the job, the only frustration that existed was the amount of bills that started pouring in and the inability to sift through and organize them."

Under cross-examination, the builder had admitted that sticky notes had been used to cover up the true amount that the construction workers had been paid. This was done by placing the sticky notes on the timecards, photocopying them, and then including the copies with the invoices sent to Sandra and the trustees. It had turned out that Sandra or her trustee had been paying labor costs based at roughly three times the rate per hour that the workers were actually receiving.

Finally, it was time for Marshal's testimony to begin. Sandra's lawyer began the questioning by asking Marshal to describe his background. Marshal recited his personal resume of education, extensive engineering experience, and professional licensure in several states. He then testified how he had first been contacted by Dale Morgan, and he described his initial impressions when first arriving at the site to meet with the trustee.

The judge stopped him there. A few days before Marshal's testimony, the judge had ordered the lawyers to speed the trial along. So after being told to speed it up, Marshal went immediately to the photographs he had taken during his inspections. As each photograph was projected onto a screen so that members of the jury could see, he pointed to the various defects using a laser pointer.

Marshal started with photographs of the front gate, pointing out how dangerous it was. Then he went on to the geotextile soil stabilizers that had been tripping hazards.

Then the lawyer stopped him, and asked if he had received the plans and specifications and had written a report in February 2001. Marshal answered that he had indeed received the plans and specifications, and he then briefly summarized what he had written in his report. Then the lawyer presented the plans to the jury while an assistant projected the images onto the screen. He then briefly discussed each sheet of plans, pointing out that the architect had not drawn structural framing plans for the second floor and the roof. Marshal then discussed the importance of the structural framing plan on a complex house like this one. He explained to the jury how he had been especially struck by the complex roofline of the house and why he had decided to begin the inspection inside the attic.

Marshal then returned to describing the various defects that he had photographed during his subsequent inspections. As each photograph came on the screen, he described how many of the wood rafters were split and improperly cut by the builder's framers. He described improper rafter seating; improperly fabricated ring beams; haphazard framing; minimal bearing of wood members onto supporting beams; lack of mechanical connectors; pulled-out members exhibiting exposed nails; large openings to the exterior; sagging in the roof; end-butted primary support beam members; discontinuous top plates; haphazard wood fillers; major beams with no connection to other members; wood support cripples butted directly against the edge of beam members with no backup blocking; strongback members used as primary beams; improper nailing throughout; discontinuous midspan cut beams and at some locations where prefabricated wood roof trusses did exist, he pointed out how the truss metal connector plates had buckled. He described how wood members had pulled away from other members, main wood cripples were wedged into stiffeners instead of being properly seated into position, and he showed missed nailing patterns as well as missing mechanical corner connectors in his photographs.

Marshal also showed photographs of the measuring devices he had installed in the attic to measure the amount of movement taking place as the roof frame rocked back and forth with the wind. He then described how the distance of movement had increased with each cycle of rocking and explained how this cyclic rocking back and forth would eventually result in total collapse of the roof.

He then discussed the second-floor truss construction and how one city inspector had told him that he had seen floor trusses that had been "chainsawed," or cut in a jagged manner. Marshal next showed the photographs he had taken of the repaired second-floor trusses above the entry foyer.

Before Marshal's testimony had begun, the motion to prevent him from testifying was settled with a lawyers' agreement that Marshal was not to speak about the forged document that he had found and that concerned the wood trusses. The lawyers would not ask him any questions about the forged truss certification letter.

Sandra's lawyers had told Marshal to look over at the jurors after he had discussed the second-floor truss construction to see if they were bored with the pictures. If they were falling asleep in their chairs, he was to cut his testimony short by eliminating the last group of pictures to show with the rest of his testimony. Marshal looked over at the jurors. To his surprise, they were wide awake! They were sitting upright, obviously growing intensely aware of what Marshal was describing in his photographs. Several of the jurors were taking notes. Marshal was later told that one of the jurors wrote, "This dream house is a nightmare!"

Then Marshal began to show photographs of the other defects including water leaks, crushed air conditioning ducts, missing electric junction box covers, crimped electric wires, exposed wires, insulation missing at some locations in the attic and unapproved cellulose insulation used in the walls, cracking in the tile floors on the second floor and in the stone arches supporting the rear decks, and water penetration through the walls and at the windows. He discussed how the fireplace hearth extensions were too narrow, a possible fire hazard, and there were no damper stops. He also discussed the cracks and gaps in the chimney flues that had been discovered by his fireplace expert who was also a City of Austin fireman. He showed photos of the numerous leak locations in the roof tiles and flashings, and he showed photos of the water staining and other water damage inside the house. He then summarized the roofing report that had been prepared by his roofing expert. He showed the photos of the defective interior millwork, including the warped French doors and improperly installed door and cabinet hardware. He also discussed the windows that would not open and the beautiful wormwood floor that had been damaged by plumbing leaks, as well as by flooding beneath the exterior doors.

The plumbing fixtures had been manufactured and shipped from France, and the fittings built within the fixtures were all of metric scale. Marshal showed photographs of how the plumbing tradesmen had installed the fixtures in the house and, instead of using adaptive gauge fittings, they had used incompatible American-gauge pipes. They had twisted the pipes into the metric fittings, splitting the fittings open, damaging the expensive fixtures, and causing the plumbing leaks that Sandra had first mentioned on late-night television.

Marshal's photographs also showed leaking propane tanks, heat-yielded metal strapping in the generator room, and hard-packed nonabsorptive rocky soil at the septic system drainfield. He showed a photograph that showed that construction debris and trucked-in rock had been used as nonpermitted fill material behind a retaining wall and covered by a thin layer of soil and grass. There were also photos of the inadequate surface drainage features, substandard driveway base materials, defective landscaping irrigation controls, and defective welding at the boat dock.

On the next day of his court appearance, Marshal completed his testimony under direct examination, and then it was time for him to face cross-examination. The builder's lawyer showed additional photographs that Marshal had taken that indicated minor, inconsequential conditions in the wood framing. As the lawyer showed the jury each photograph, he asked Marshal if he had been exaggerating the nature of the problems at the house. He felt the lawyer's efforts to discredit his testimony were weak because the jury could see for themselves the poor construction quality from the photographs that he had shown the jury the day before.

The lawyer also attacked Marshal's professionalism by accusing Marshal of being "highly unprofessional" and "too extreme." Nevertheless, Marshal remained calm and described the fact that Sandra Bullock had also retained another engineer to conduct a peer review of his work, and the engineer acknowledged the fact that Marshal's work was indeed professional and well reasoned. Marshal also explained that it was the scientific evidence that he had also provided—consisting of calculations, measurements, and reference to engineering technical literature—that made his testimony irrefutable. He had read the reports prepared by the builder's own engineering experts, and he knew that once those experts had testified, Sandra's lawyer would point out that they had already agreed with Marshal's position. Even the opposing engineers had agreed that the house was a "nightmare."

During a lunch break, Marshal asked Sandra how she was holding up. During the trial, other unhappy homeowners had testified about their defective homes and their previous experiences with the builder. Here she was, fighting about something that all of them as homebuyers had seemingly gotten trapped into. She had tried to build a home in Texas where many homebuyers suffer from builders who take advantage of lack of licensing requirements and lack of regulation of the homebuilding industry, and also suffer from what had become Governor Rick Perry's version of "tort reform." Had Sandra's builder been more astute, he would have forced her and her trustee to incorporate an enforceable, mandatory binding arbitration clause into their agreement, which would have eliminated her constitutional right to even sue in court to bring her case before a jury.

Sandra was genuinely angry at what had happened to her, but she was equally angry at what she had seen other homebuyers go through. She had been considering establishing a charitable foundation to help other homebuyers in Texas who had been abused by their builders. This was a noble gesture, but Marshal stated that she should think it through. For one thing, she had been able to exert her constitutional rights to a trial by jury, whereas tens of thousands of Texas homebuyers were faced with having to go through binding arbitration. Marshal knew that it was going to be very difficult politically to get mandatory binding arbitration removed from contracts in Texas. In fact it might take future federal legislation to accomplish the task because the large national homebuilders were just too politically powerful in Texas. He knew her proposed charitable foundation would be inundated with requests for help from tens of thousands of Texas homebuyers and that it would be quickly drained of its funds. Also, the Texas Residential Construction Commission had been enacted by the Texas Legislature in 2003 and had been sold to the Legislature as a homebuyer protection agency. However, it was rapidly becoming known as a *builder* protection agency as established under Governor Perry. At least Sandra Bullock had a chance at resolution, but there was little hope for the rest of the people buying defective houses in Texas.

Then Marshal simply said to Sandra, "You know, it can't be fixed—your house. The repair contractor has estimated that it would cost more to repair what is there than it would cost just to tear it down and start over. The cost of repair is too great. Win, lose, or draw, just bulldoze the main house to the ground, but try to salvage as many materials as you possibly can and give them to charity. At least the concrete foundation is in reasonably good shape, but that's the only thing in the main house that is. But be sure to keep the guesthouse."

On that note, he stood up to return to the courtroom, complimented Sandra on her fortitude, and told her goodbye. Marshal testified again that afternoon, and then he was finished. He shook the hands of Sandra's father and the lawyers as he left the courtroom. As he was walking to the elevator he saw that four well-dressed Chinese men had followed him from the courtroom. As he entered the elevator, he saw that the other men had headed toward the staircase. Marshal would recall those men many years later.

Several months before the trial had begun, the Bullock trustee had also hired a Boston architect-engineering firm to conduct more extensive removal of wall materials in an effort to determine the problems with the window and door flashings and other water intrusion sources. The architect testified to the incredible amount of water intrusion due to lack of window flashings and defectively installed rock work, stucco, and roofing materials. He also testified that he had found toxic stachybotrus mold in the house.

The trial continued for several more weeks. The architect-builder who had built the house, apparently lacking justification for his company's actions, reportedly tried to deflect his actions away from himself and his company by verbally attacking his superintendent and his subcontractors and filing lawsuits against some of them. He claimed that they were the ones to blame for the poor quality of construction.

Finally on October 14, 2004, after eight weeks of trial, it was over. The jury returned a verdict in Sandra's favor of over $6.5 million. She then said to *People* magazine, "I felt firmly committed to see the process through, especially for all of those homeowners who could never afford to come this far." About two years later, she tore the house down. The salvageable materials were given away to charity or recycled.

After Marshal had completed his testimony and was driving back to his office, a nagging thought kept entering his mind: *Why would someone assert that I am unprofessional?* Opposing lawyers could always be expected to criticize an expert's analysis in as critical a manner as possible, but after decades of investigating building failures and causes of personal injuries, and having met at least a hundred lawyers in his work, no lawyer on either side of the table had ever accused him of being unprofessional. When the lawyer asserted to the jury at this particular trial that Marshal was unprofessional, Marshal had been taken aback. His immediate thought had been, *Where did that come from?*

As Marshal drove in his car, he kept thinking, *Is somebody trying to damage my reputation? And if so, for what purpose?* Marshal arrived at his destination at the Scarbrough Building, exited the elevator at the ninth floor, and approached his office door. As he entered his office he thought, *Probably that lawyer was just losing his case and got carried away in the heat of the moment.*

With time, Marshal simply forgot about it.

Almost three years would pass before Marshal would recall that moment. He had not known that his testimony in the Sandra Bullock case had made him a target of some very wealthy and powerful people. During Marshal's drive back to his office after completing his testimony, he was totally unaware that preparations were being made to prevent him from ever successfully testifying against a homebuilder or anyone else ever again.

8

CR TWO AMENDMENTS DOWN RO

Marshal handed his briefcase to Myrtle and instructed her to empty it into the Bullock house file. "See to it that everything that belongs to Sandra or the trustee is returned to them; then mark the file 'closed' and ship it to the warehouse," he said.

"Marshal," Myrtle said, "you need to read that letter that I placed on your desk."

Marshal left his office door open, walked to his desk, and picked up the letter. It was a letter that a homebuilder's lawyer had sent to Mrs. R. V. Davis, who was one of Marshal's clients. He slowly sat down in his chair while reading:

> Dear Mrs. Davis:
> I am an attorney representing Gehamma Home Corporation. As you know, the home that you purchased in my client's subdivision is located across the street from my client's field office and model home. I have been told that two prospective purchasers crossed the street and knocked on your door. One of our representatives followed them and overheard what you told them. You reportedly told the prospective purchasers that there are homes with foundation failures on your end of the subdivision. You said that your 'patience has now run out' and that

you 'intend to prevent Gehamma from cheating anyone else out of their savings.' This is a demand that you immediately cease and desist from presenting any false information to others pertaining to your home or the subdivision, particularly the false comments about foundation failures in your subdivision. The builder respects your constitutional right to free speech. However, spreading false information goes well beyond free speech. Instead, it constitutes intentional and tortious conduct. If you insist on making statements to others, we insist that you be truthful. Should you speak or write any such false information, we will view it as evidence of tortious conduct, including liable, slander, false-light, tortious interference, and wrongful business disparagement, and we will file a lawsuit against you.

Marshal set the letter on his desk and began working on his computer, taking notes as he went. After about thirty minutes he said, "Myrtle, would you come in here for a moment, please?" Myrtle grabbed a notepad, walked into Marshal's office, and sat in a chair in front of his desk.

"Myrtle, this letter from Gehamma's lawyer to our client, Mrs. Davis, is a threat to try to keep her from telling the truth about all of the foundation failures in her part of her subdivision. She was threatened just because some prospective homebuyers wanted to make a wise purchase and not just listen to the palaver that they were getting from the salesmen who work in that model home. That builder knows that he placed those foundations on top of an active spring and that there are foundations failing throughout that entire end of the subdivision. We have here a large building corporation that is threatening an individual homebuyer, who now knows that if she doesn't stay silent, she will have to spend a lot of money on a defense lawyer just for telling the truth about the condition of her home, as well as the condition of her neighbors' homes."

"I've already telephoned Mrs. Davis and gotten the story from her," Myrtle said. "She and her neighbors have been raising a storm about their houses, and the builder is trying to shut them up so that they can finish building out the subdivision and sell their crummy houses to other people. She can't sue the builder because they signed binding arbitration agreements. They are now going through the process involving that new state agency, the Texas Residential Construction Commission, or TRCC. I told her that she should still hire a lawyer. I mentioned that I had read that companies that manufacture defective products routinely threaten scores of Web sites and blogs that review consumer products and services. Those companies routinely lose many of the cases that go to court, but Mrs. Davis said she just didn't have enough money to pay a lawyer to fight."

"So what we seem to have here," said Marshal, "are at least three constitutional issues—two of which relate to the First Amendment and the other relates to the Seventh Amendment. To truncate it, the First Amendment states that 'Congress shall make no law . . . abridging the freedom of speech . . .'

"On the one hand we have a homebuilder corporation's perceived right to tell prospective buyers falsehoods about the condition of the homes that they build. On the other hand we have an individual's right to tell the truth, albeit at tremendous personal expense to that individual, because if the corporation files suit against the individual for telling the truth, then the corporation can crush that individual with the costs of litigation.

"Corporations were granted the legal status of a 'person' many years ago, so one must ask 'If that's the case, what kind of person is it?' Antisocial? Self-interested? Inherently amoral? Callous? Deceitful? You can routinely read in the newspapers how another corporate officer forgot the ethics lessons he learned in kindergarten.

"As corporations partner with our government, I'll bet that one day in the near future, the United States Supreme Court will rule that corporations as well as government union organizations have the constitutional right to free speech, and they will be able to spend as much money as they want on politics as if corporate or union entities were citizens with a guaranteed voice in an election. The monopolistic corporations will take the money out of the profits they make from overpricing their products, and the government unions will take the money out of the taxpayer. With corporations and government labor bosses being able to control what you say, they will also be able to control what you think, and at election time both groups will pour money into the mainstream media to warp the truth about any bought-and-paid-for politician that they want to get elected. The individual American will be enslaved with no liberties by a nonrepresentative form of government."

"Marshal," Myrtle said, "where have you been? One way or the other, they get that money to the politicians no matter what."

"All right," said Marshal. "I get your point, but Mrs. Davis's letter brings up a second constitutional issue—the right to trial by jury in a civil case. She agreed to enter binding arbitration in her sales contract because if she didn't sign the contract containing that provision, then they would not have sold the house to her in the first place. She just didn't know what she was buying. One thing that Sandra Bullock and her lawyers told me was that she had learned that there are a lot of homebuyers in trouble who are having problems with binding arbitration, and as a result they can't get their cases to court. Bullock's lawyers also told me about all of the homebuyer complaints concerning the TRCC. They said it was known as a 'builder protection agency.'

"Myrtle, the right to trial by jury in a civil case is addressed by the Seventh Amendment to the United States Constitution, which provides: 'In Suits at common law, where the value in controversy shall exceed twenty dollars, the right of trial by jury shall be preserved, and no fact tried by a jury shall be otherwise re-examined in any Court of the United States, than according to the rules of the common law.' Joseph Story's 1833 treatise, *Commentaries on the Constitution of the United States*, reads, 'It is a most important and valuable amendment; and places upon the high ground of constitutional right the inestimable privilege of a trial by jury in civil cases, a privilege scarcely inferior to that in criminal cases, which is conceded by all to be essential to political and civil liberty.'"

"Marshal," Myrtle said, "I can tell that you didn't memorize that. You have your eyes on your computer monitor."

"True, my dear Myrtle." Marshal said. "It's amazing how you can find just what you're looking for on the Web. But the real issue is how homebuyers have had their Seventh Amendment rights taken away from them when they buy a house. Arbitration is a dispute-resolution process that usually involves a single individual who sits as a judge and who might not even have any background in the practice of law. It's a very expensive process. The two parties get together in a room with their lawyers, present their cases, and the decision of that arbitrator is final as if there had been a trial. There are appeals possible as a result of a trial; however, with few exceptions there are no appeals to the decision of an arbitrator.

"The use of mandatory binding arbitration is widespread in the new-home industry. At least ninety percent of the nation's top builders require mandatory binding arbitration in their contracts or in their warranty agreements. Some lawyers consider this industrywide practice to be a restraint of trade when buyers have no choice, such as in The Woodlands outside Houston where most if not all builders include binding arbitration in their non-negotiable contracts. If you want to buy a new house in The Woodlands, you are forced to agree to binding arbitration to settle disputes, which cuts off your access to a court of law."

"Well, thanks to the slave wages you pay me, I'm not rich enough to retire to The Woodlands," said Myrtle.

"Myrtle, you earn almost as much as I do, and you know it. You're also my bookkeeper, and you write out my paycheck. I'm trying to say that it doesn't matter how big or small a house you buy; the vast majority of builders have inserted arbitration clauses into their contracts. Builders are using the contract forms developed by the Texas Association of Builders that include the arbitration clauses, and that organization has said that twenty percent of its members build eighty percent of the new homes in Texas. They also say that almost all of their members utilize arbitration clauses in their contracts. You as a homebuyer are forced to surrender your constitutional rights to trial by jury in order to live in a nice neighborhood, and as far as the large homebuilders are concerned, if you don't like it you can live somewhere else. Big corporations can now control where you live.

"Which gets me to the third constitutional issue at stake here. Sandra Bullock's lawyers told me about all of the homebuyer complaints concerning the TRCC state agency becoming known as a 'builder protection agency.' Remember that the First Amendment states, 'Congress shall make no law . . . abridging . . . the right of the people . . . to petition the Government for a redress of grievances.' In 2003, the Texas Legislature created the bill requiring Texas homebuyers to petition the TRCC for a redress of their grievances, and Governor Rick Perry signed that bill into law that year touting it as 'tort reform.' That means that homebuyers must present their house's defect issues to a state bureaucracy that protects homebuilders and that has no mandate to treat homebuyers with any semblance of due process."

"I don't think tort reform is all it's cracked up to be," said Myrtle. "What I've heard is that business and insurance corporations were able to use exaggerated or made-up cases to illustrate their points and then they got Governor Perry to do their bidding. I've heard that tort reform is really the creation of corporate special interests who seek to immunize themselves from liability. My niece is a lawyer, and she tells me that tort reform is a two-word catchphrase that regular people barely understand and that is based on the incorrect assumption that it's easy and common to sue anyone for anything. She says that most judges throw out the flaky claims before they even get started and no lawyer wants to take a case that is a guaranteed loser."

"I agree," said Marshal, "but getting disputes settled through a bureaucratic process is worse. Take a look. I've printed out this article written by George Leef, citing Robert A. Levy and William Mellor, that describes how agency bureaucrats now write the laws that regulate our lives instead of Congress. It says, 'The Constitution does not say that Congress is allowed to turn its lawmaking authority over to bureaucrats, but it has been doing so for many years. Naturally, the Supreme Court has been willing to acquiesce in that, believing that Congress needs to rely on administrative experts to make lots of regulations to control our lives.' The 2001 case, *Whitman v. American Trucking Associations, Inc.,* 'was an opportunity for the Court to apply the brakes on bureaucratic lawmaking, but it went the other way, tearing up what remained of the nondelegation principle. The justices ruled that delegation of lawmaking authority is permissible even if the standards set forth for the agency to follow are extremely vague.' On the federal level, government agency bureaucrats who we don't elect now write the laws that regulate our lives; and those bureaucrats are unionized, so they can't even be fired.

"Here in Texas we have a state agency, the Texas Residential Construction Commission that controls the lives of homebuyers. However, the Texas Constitution has a strict separation of powers. In Texas, agencies are only supposed to apply laws, not write them. So just who are the people behind the establishment of the TRCC who intend to control the lives of homebuyers with bureaucratic form-filing procedures and vague, nonengineered construction-compliance standards that TRCC is setting up?

"To begin with, there is the Texas Association of Builders that pushed the bill through the Legislature in the name of tort reform so that their members could benefit financially. But then it had to go to Governor Perry's desk for him to sign. It's on the governor's desk where I believe the government–corporation partnership has come together. Myrtle, you're probably old enough to remember what President Dwight Eisenhower said in 1961 about the military–industrial complex as he was leaving office."

"Marshal . . ." Myrtle growled. She knew that Marshal was aware that she did not like to be reminded of her age.

"Sorry, Myrtle. Just kidding," Marshal said. "Here, I've printed a part of what Ike said. He said:

> Until the latest of our world conflicts, the United States had no armaments industry. American makers of plowshares could, with time and as required, make swords as well. But now we can no longer risk emergency improvisation of national defense; we have been compelled to create a permanent armaments industry of vast proportions. Added to this, three and a half million men and women are directly engaged in the defense establishment. We annually spend on

military security more than the net income of all United States corporations.

In the councils of government, we must guard against the acquisition of unwarranted influence, whether sought or unsought, by the military–industrial complex. The potential for the disastrous rise of misplaced power exists and will persist.

We must never let the weight of this combination endanger our liberties or democratic processes. We should take nothing for granted. Only an alert and knowledgeable citizenry can compel the proper meshing of the huge industrial and military machinery of defense with our peaceful methods and goals, so that security and liberty may prosper together.

"Now, I believe what President Eisenhower was also saying was that we Americans must remain alert and knowledgeable about the dangers of big corporations and big government working together in partnerships. In alliance, they are able to bring about a powerful force that endangers our individual liberties, including our democratic processes.

"Here, I want to show you something I recorded the other day. Have you seen the Swift Boat television ads that are being run to benefit President George W. Bush in his presidential campaign against U.S. Senator John Kerry? They make Kerry look pretty bad."

"You don't need to show the ad, Marshal," said Myrtle. "I've seen the ads already, but I've wondered who was paying for them."

"I looked into that, Myrtle, before I asked you to come in and sit down just now. According to news sources, a big homebuilder in San Antonio, Tex Prairie, is paying for much of it, but I don't know who else is involved. He's head of Prairie Homes and is considered one of the more successful homebuilders in Texas. He seems to be providing much of the funding for the Swift Boat advertisements.

"According to the articles I found, for about two decades, Tex Prairie has used his multimillion dollar fortune to fund the Republican revolution both in Texas and nationally. In 1986, Tex Prairie became a finance co-chairman for the Texas gubernatorial campaign of Republican Bill Clements. By that time, the war between homebuilders and homebuyers had already been long and costly, particularly to the homebuilders. In the 1970s, the Democrat-controlled Texas Legislature passed the Texas Deceptive Trade Practices Act, known as 'DTPA,' which allowed homebuyers to sue their builders for house defects and receive treble damage awards. If a person bought a house from a builder for 50,000 dollars and could prove that defects existed in the house, that person could receive a 150,000-dollar judgment against the builder and still keep the house. For a time, certainly from the homebuilders' perspective, there appeared to be a bounty on homebuilders in Texas.

"The Carter-era Monetary Control Act of 1980 eliminated the barriers that had previously protected the states from the New York–based megabanking industry, allowing the financiers to cross state lines and charge usurious interest rates on borrowed money in every state. This is what led directly to our national debt getting completely out of control in the mid-1980s and could soon lead to an overwhelming financial crisis. If you've ever read Karl Marx, he wrote that it was financial usury that brought about the French Revolution. Since the mid-1980s, the United States has been continuously in debt and barely able to pay even the interest on the debt to other nations, particularly China. The consolidation of the banking industry was then achieved by the federal government working together with the largest banks that were deemed by the government to be 'too big to fail.'

"Also by the mid-1980s, Republicans began to gain momentum in Texas politics for the first time since the Civil War. The 1970s tax-and-spend policies of the Democrat-controlled Congress, implementation of the Environmental Protection Agency and windfall profit taxes on petroleum-based products, and the FDIC- and Federal Reserve–engineered economic collapse that took place in Texas in the 1980s all resulted in the flight of manufacturing and industry to overseas locations. The individual fortunes of most of the Texas bankers were decimated as were the fortunes of most of the large and small Texas homebuilders. These actions left a large void in capital restructuring and formation for small, medium, and large businesses within the

Texas economy, thereby enabling New York–based multistate banks and large Wall Street–financed homebuilders to enter Texas, seize assets through the FDIC, and by the early 1990s dominate the capital distribution and construction of billions of dollars' worth of new homes in Texas.

"In 1986, Karl Rove, adviser to President George W. Bush, reportedly convinced Tex Prairie to help raise money to rebuild the Texas Republican Party. Rove also raised funds to help launch the Texas Civil Justice League, a group that carried the message that trial lawyers are bad people who are wrecking the business climate with frivolous lawsuits. Then Rove helped expand the Citizens Against Lawsuit Abuse group which also hammered on the same theme. Rove was also involved with another group called Texans for Lawsuit Reform that involved a number of politicians involved with U.S. House Majority Leader Tom Delay and the raising of money for the 2002 elections.

"In 2003, Governor Perry, who had changed his political affiliation from Democrat to Republican in 1988 evidently to enhance his political ambitions, called three consecutive special legislative sessions to enable a congressional redistricting plan more favorable to Republicans. The plan was finally adopted and was supported by U.S. House Majority Leader Tom DeLay, bringing about a five-seat Republican gain in the delegation.

"Also in 2003, a fellow named Sam Kruger, who was the corporate counsel of Prairie Homes, reportedly helped draft much of the legislation that passed the Texas Legislature and established the TRCC. Governor Perry then signed the legislation into law in the name of tort reform. The most employer-related contributions for Rick Perry's run for governor had been raised by Prairie Home's Sam Kruger, and Governor Perry in turn appointed Kruger to the newly established TRCC.

"As you might recall, Rick Perry had been elected lieutenant governor of Texas in 1998. He assumed office as governor in December 2000 when then-Governor George W. Bush resigned before his inauguration as president of the United States. In 2002, while seeking his first four-year term as governor, Governor Perry raised and spent about 25 million dollars, which was enough to defeat his Democratic challenger.

"President Eisenhower warned us about the military–industrial complex. Now I'm beginning to suspect that here in Texas under Governor Perry we have a modern-day government–corporate complex that has manifested itself as a partnership between the Texas Residential Construction Commission and the giant homebuilding corporations that monopolize the vast majority of home construction in the state.

"Myrtle," Marshal said, "pull Mrs. Davis's file and make a note for me to finalize my report to her. Please emphasize that I have already determined that foundation failures do exist at that end of the subdivision, in case that corporate builder chooses to file a slander suit against her. She'll need to hire a lawyer, and I want to get that letter to her just in case. However, I doubt anything more will come of it because I'm sure that Mrs. Davis has been scared into silence while the builder continues to build out that subdivision and then sells its houses to other unfortunate people, and then moves on."

9

ᴄ🙌 A Learned Treatise 🙌

Between 2003—the year in which Governor Rick Perry signed the bill creating the Texas Residential Construction Commission—and 2007, homebuilders sold an estimated 400,000 new homes in Texas, and thousands of new subdivisions dotted the Texas landscape.

A number of those new subdivisions contained the less-desirable highly expansive clay soils found throughout much of Central, East, and South Texas. Many of the major interstate homebuilders built their houses on substandard concrete foundations that utilized stress steel cables and were the cheapest foundations possible. As the soil would expand and contract with the change in seasons, the foundations would move with the ground. It was only after walls began to buckle and crack, doors started to jam open or closed, or the foundation would start to crack that Marshal and other professional engineers would be asked to look at a particular house that was already in trouble.

Governor Perry's version of tort reform as well as binding arbitration had stopped almost all lawsuits against homebuilders, so most homebuilders simply ignored most of the homebuyers' complaints, telling them to contact the TRCC.

Whenever Marshal's existing clients would see evidence of a structural deficiency in their houses and builders had refused to make repairs, Marshal's clients would contact him for an opinion. Marshal would counsel them that he had learned from other engineers that the homeowners simply could not win against the builders because they had signed an arbitration agreement with the builder and had bargained away their constitutional rights to go to court. He had heard that most lawyers would not take these kinds of cases any longer. Marshal would tell them to fix their houses as best they could and chalk up their losses as the "way things are." He would counsel new clients in the same manner.

Many of Marshal's clients refused to listen to his advice, hoping instead that they might still have some semblance of constitutional rights in Texas. They would then choose to try the TRCC method that would eventually lead to arbitration. Marshal found that many of his clients behaved this way out of desperation because many of them were young or middle-age couples with children, who had invested their life savings into their houses. Because most of the structural deficiencies were related to the flimsy foundations that the builder had constructed on expansive clay soils, in most instances Marshal would advise that the foundations simply could not be fixed at a reasonable price.

Some homebuyers found that they had no choice other than to try to get their homebuilders to buy the houses back. Homebuilders are in business to sell houses, and Marshal's clients soon learned that homebuilders would not buy the houses back, in part because the builders could not properly repair the defective foundations any better than could the homebuyers. Besides, the larger builders were riding a wave of subdivision development, homebuilding, and financial manipulation that was encompassing the entire nation. The builders ignored the complaining homebuyers, choosing instead to dedicate their time to building as many houses as possible. Then the builders would sell other houses to the next buyers, making as much money along the way as possible before leaving the country ahead of the inevitable economic collapse.

With its power to inspect and opine on the condition of a house before a homebuyer's arbitration process could begin, the TRCC provided the necessary delays that benefitted the homebuilders. When the homebuyer would file a claim with TRCC, the agency would send out their inspectors who would spend a lot of time interpreting standards, filling out forms, delaying for a year or two, and then finally refusing to admit that there was anything wrong with the house. The TRCC also had the power to categorize a complaint as "legitimate," and a number of complaints were never even acknowledged as such. The process delayed any sense of justice for the homebuyers while the homebuilders continued to build out their subdivisions in Texas.

By 2005, after only two years in existence, state representatives were beginning to hear complaints from many Texas homebuyers about the TRCC process. The homebuilders then reinforced their influence over state affairs by providing vast sums of money to Perry and the lawmakers. Many Texas lawmakers benefitted from almost $3 million given by one Texas homebuilder. This single homebuilder accounted for seventy-two percent of the $4 million in political contributions tracked by the watchdog group Texans for Public Justice. One report indicated that the same homebuilder contributed more than $21 million to political candidates and judges. Various builders gave in excess of $600,000 to Perry. Only six Texas legislators, all Democrats, did not receive any homebuilder "political contributions"—the semi-Orwellian phrase that commonly replaces the word "bribe."

Rick Perry was elected to full gubernatorial terms in 2002 and 2006. As a result, according to the *Dallas Morning News*, Perry acquired the distinction of being the only governor in modern Texas history to have appointed at least one person to every possible state office, board, or commission to which a governor of Texas can appoint someone. Those people include several of Perry's appointees to the Texas Board of Professional Engineers, enough to comprise the majority of the Board.

In the early days of the TRCC, Perry saw to it that Texas A&M received a minimum of $45,000 to develop new evaluation standards for TRCC's inspectors to follow. Two lawyers working for Texas A&M wrote the standards with minimal, if any, input from professional engineers. The standards were written in a way that builders would not be required to make repairs. Much later, Perry saw to it that $50 million was transferred from another state fund for the construction of new buildings at Texas A&M.

In 2006, the Texas Comptroller of Public Accounts wrote:

> The majority of homeowners who responded to my survey are disappointed and angry that the costly and bureaucratic TRCC process does nothing to ensure their construction defects are fixed. Thus, their only recourse is binding arbitration, as required by most builder contracts, or go to court, precisely the outcome the act was created to prevent. It appears that the act and TRCC rules simply create additional roadblocks for homeowners seeking relief.
>
> After reviewing TRCC and its enabling statute, it is clear that the agency functions as a builder protection agency. Inspectors use TRCC's building and performance standards to determine the validity of a homeowner's claim of a defect. Either party may file a claim and a TRCC-registered third-party inspector will be assigned to inspect the alleged defect. The inspector will refer to the performance standards and state-mandated limited warranties to evaluate the alleged defect and, if a defect is confirmed, recommend a repair. Inspector training documents from TRCC prohibit registered third-party inspectors from mentioning or including an item in an inspection report that was not included in the claim, unless the defect is a health and safety issue.

The "third-party inspectors" permitted to address health and safety issues were independent professional engineers who were supposed to be free from the influence of homebuyers and homebuilders. Initially many of the professional engineers did what was expected of them. However, in order to become a third-party inspector working on behalf of the TRCC, professional engineers had to be "pre-approved" by TRCC, effectively placing the engineer's performance and decisions under the control of TRCC. By statute, the only state agency with the power to regulate professional engineers is the Texas Board of Professional Engineers. Nevertheless, TRCC's highly irregular power grab over its third-party inspectors went mysteriously unopposed by the Texas Board of Professional Engineers.

There were no assurances given to any pre-approved third-party engineer that he or she would receive any work from TRCC; nevertheless, it soon became apparent that those engineers willing to compromise their ethics and provide engineering reports that benefitted homebuilders would be assured of receiving additional work from TRCC. Texas taxpayers paid an estimated $10 million per year financing third-party inspection reports that benefitted homebuilders in this manner.

Some of Marshal Yeager's clients had no choice other than proceed through the TRCC process and see what happened. Marshal agreed to assist a young couple who had bought a house from a builder. The house had a garage foundation that was settling and about to break away from the house. Marshal discovered that the garage portion of the house had been built over an old creek bed that the builder had filled with loose dirt shortly before constructing the foundation, and the foundation had settled into the loose fill.

The TRCC sent out its selected third-party engineering inspector who wrote a report that would require the homebuilder to stabilize the foundation of the garage and prevent it from settling in the future. The homebuilder, not wanting to make the repairs, filed an appeal with TRCC objecting that the third-party engineer's assessment was "incorrect, insufficient, and not reasonable under the circumstances."

The TRCC Appellate Panel, which included two state-employed professional engineers, then referred to other reports prepared by the homebuilder's engineers that had incorporated false, builder-favorable measurements. Then a TRCC panel member telephoned the third-party engineering inspector and told the engineer to "clarify" his measurements and, in effect, rewrite his report in a manner that would be favorable to the builder. It was implied that should the engineer refuse to change his report, he might not be allowed to conduct additional TRCC inspections in the future. The engineer then changed his report, and the TRCC Appellate Panel subsequently ruled against the homebuyers, stating that the builder was not required to make repairs.

Unbeknownst to TRCC's third-party inspector or any of the engineers on the TRCC Appellate Panel, the young couple, acting under Marshal's advice, had witnessed and secretly videotaped the TRCC third-party engineer's actions during his inspection at their house. The video showed the engineer making the measurements in a correct manner. When Marshal learned that the TRCC had threatened its own third-party engineer and that he had indeed changed his report, Marshal advised his clients as well as TRCC that he intended to report the activities of TRCC, the professional engineers involved, and the homebuilder to the district attorney's office and the Federal Bureau of Investigation.

Marshal's uncalculated misstep in telling TRCC his plans led to what happened next. By threatening to blow the whistle to the authorities about the illegal activities involving TRCC, the homebuilders, and the engineers, Marshal Yeager had inadvertently exposed himself as an obvious threat to the Texas political establishment in Austin. Unbeknownst to Marshal, the trap for him had already been set, and Marshal, along with the three members of the DeBarberie family, were about to become victims of the unconstitutional corporate state.

In 2006, a year before Marshal told TRCC his plans, a woman named Angela DeBarberie had gone through the terrible ordeal of losing her sixty-two-year-old mother in an automobile accident. Angela and her husband, Todd DeBarberie, then faced the added responsibility of taking care of Angela's disabled sixty-five-year-old father. Angela's father, Howard Erickson, sustained injuries from the notorious Charles Whitman sniper attack in Austin in 1966, and he required special living accommodations—especially a bathroom with a shower that would accommodate his wheelchair. Angela then moved her father into their small home in San Antonio and sold her parents' house in Dallas. She and Todd debated whether to add another bedroom and handicap-accessible bathroom to their home, or build a new house to accommodate all of their needs. The DeBarberies already owned a ten-acre tract of raw land about twenty-five miles north of San Antonio, located off a rural county road in the gently rolling, tall-grass-covered hills of Central Texas. They had intended to build their retirement home there someday, but now they thought about how wonderful it would be for Howard to be able to sit on a porch and enjoy the sunsets over the beautiful terrain.

The sale of Angela's parents' house in Dallas generated $300,000 cash, so the DeBarberies set out to find an architect to design the new home. The architect designed a small, two-story wood-frame house with stone veneer, lapped cement board siding, vinyl covered single-hung windows, and a tall, pitched, standing-seam metal roof, highlighted by two dormers set into the roof above the front porch. The first floor contained a main entry area, family room, dining room, full kitchen, master bathroom and bedroom with walk-in closets, a tile shower, and a whirlpool bathtub. The second floor contained additional bedrooms, walk-in closets, and another bathroom. The architect included an additional, smaller house structure that would accommodate Howard's special needs. That house included an accessible kitchen, accessible cabinets, family room, bedroom, and a bathroom that included an accessible shower with a floor that would accommodate Howard's wheelchair.

A large open breezeway separated the two house structures and also interconnected the front and back porches. Instead of carpet, tile, or hardwood floors, the DeBarberies wanted stained and etched concrete floors throughout all living areas as well as at the porches and breezeway.

The architect retained a structural engineer to provide design drawings for a conventional-rebar concrete slab on ground foundation system, which is a widely used type of foundation system utilized in the southern and western parts of the United States. The structural engineer depicted separate foundations for each house structure, with a long expansion joint through the breezeway to separate the two foundation slabs from each other. The joint was necessary to prevent cracking that could result from expansion and contraction of the foundation system caused by ambient temperature extremes. The joint was to be concealed by the bottom of a stone veneer wall located along one side of the breezeway.

With the architect's plans in hand, the DeBarberies set out to find a contractor. A friend in their church, who had a brother-in-law who knew a man who had heard about a building contractor, put the DeBarberies in touch with Sline Construction Company.

Mr. Randolph Sline showed up at the DeBarberies property, a short man, cleanly dressed, very polite, and full of stories about the many beautiful homes he had built over the past twenty years in a town in another state. When the DeBarberies asked for references, Sline explained how his ex-wife had "kept the business records and photographs of all of those houses during their divorce proceedings" and therefore he was "unable to provide any proof of his accomplishments." But he did say that he and his ex-wife were "getting along better now," and he should be able to provide some verification of his credentials "sometime in the near future."

Texas is a wide-open, freewheeling state when it comes to homebuilders, with no state or county building codes or construction regulations outside the limits of Texas municipalities. Construction and inspection requirements for rural and semirural areas of the state range from few to none. With the state lacking regulation and licensure of homebuilders, anyone can be a homebuilder in Texas, including Randolph Sline, who failed to mention his recent felony conviction, incarceration, and the fact that he was now out on parole.

Sline stated that he would need to place a mechanics lien on the DeBarberies property in order to arrange for the interim financing at a bank, where he could borrow money to build the house. The DeBarberies signed the necessary papers. One clause in the agreement required the DeBarberies to utilize binding arbitration in the event any dispute should arise. Ultimately, this act would prove to be an unfortunate mistake.

The DeBarberies gave Sline $5,000 to get started. Sline cleared the grass and other vegetation from the site so that he could begin construction of the foundations. Sline then told the DeBarberies that there was a delay at the bank that was to provide the interim financing and that the DeBarberies would need to provide him with additional cash advances so that he could pay his workers and buy supplies. The DeBarberies gave Sline an additional $10,000.

Construction proceeded slowly. Most weekdays no one was on the site building anything. Sline said he needed more money. Then the DeBarberies gave Sline an additional $10,000, and then an additional $10,000 after that. After several months of sporadic construction and further cash demands by Sline, the DeBarberies realized that they had given Sline almost all of their $300,000, and the house wasn't even half finished.

Although Angela and Todd knew little about house construction, Todd did have some knowledge of electrical wiring. While Sline's workers were installing the wiring, Todd saw that the wiring was much too small and would most likely cause a fire once the permanent electricity was turned on.

The DeBarberies had never seen Sline on the job supervising his workers. None of the workers could speak or read English. Todd was able to speak some broken "Tex-Mex" and was able to learn that all of the workers on the job were undocumented workers from Mexico being paid substandard wages by Sline. None of the workers were licensed tradespeople. Todd then confronted Sline about the slow pace of the work as well as the quality of work already done. For a day, Sline accelerated construction of the exterior stone veneer in an effort to conceal deficiencies within the walls. Todd then fired Sline and ordered him off the property.

Sline countered by filing suit against the DeBarberies for an additional $50,000 that he claimed he was owed. Because Sline still retained a mechanics lien on the DeBarberies' property, there was nothing the DeBarberies could do other than pay him an additional $50,000 to get the lien released or face binding arbitration. They chose arbitration, and so Sline was able to prevent the DeBarberies from hiring another contractor to undo the defective construction because his mechanics lien would be superior to the lien required by another contractor.

The DeBarberies hired a lawyer, Russell Goodguy, who in turn contacted Marshal, asking him if he was interested in inspecting the project and giving him an evaluation of the engineering conditions that existed at the site. The lawyer told Marshal that no work had taken place at the site for several months. Marshal agreed to drive to the site to conduct an inspection.

Marshal and Angela scheduled a time to meet, and when Marshal arrived at the house, he met inside the partially completed house with Angela and her father Howard, who was sitting in his wheelchair. Marshal could see that he and Howard were about the same age.

"My daughter and son-in-law swept the wood blocks and wires and other debris that was inside here so that I could accompany you around, at least inside the house," Howard said. "There's too much debris outside, so I won't be able to accompany you out there in this wheelchair. You've got a fine reputation, Marshal. I'm the one paying the bills, so please send your invoice addressed to me."

Marshal thanked Howard for the compliment. "You look vaguely familiar to me," Marshal said. "Have we met before?"

"If we've ever met before, it must have been a very long time ago," Howard said.

Marshal could see that the house was not even half finished, and construction debris indeed littered the exterior area but the interior of the house was reasonably clean. Marshal conducted his inspection, noting extensive framing deficiencies, a cracked foundation, misaligned and bent window frames, improperly anchored stone masonry veneer, and polyvinyl chloride water pipes with glued joint fittings that a previous inspector had found located within the concrete foundation slab—with the potential for future water leakage. Marshal also found signs of roof leaks.

Using his cell phone, Marshal contacted the structural engineer who had designed the foundation. The engineer said that Sline had not wanted to pay him to conduct inspections of the reinforcing steel before the concrete was poured, so he had no idea if the reinforcing steel had been placed correctly. He confirmed that he had not used the stress steel cable system that is blamed for so many problems with house foundations. Because the construction was outside the municipal city limits of nearby towns, no governmental inspections had been performed.

The status of the law at the time of the DeBarberie/Sline agreement was such that Sline had the DeBarberies by the throat, but after many months of delays the TRCC had finally permitted the

DeBarberies to bring their case to a local arbitrator.

The arbitration hearing process is similar to that of a courtroom setting but is more private and informal, and it is usually conducted in the arbitrator's conference room. The arbitrator is usually an impartial lawyer or sometimes a retired judge. There is no jury. Each party is given an equal amount of time to present his or her case and present witnesses. Those witnesses can be questioned by the arbitrator and by the lawyers. Then the arbitrator takes a recess to determine a verdict. The recess can take a few minutes or the arbitrator can wait days or weeks after the hearing is closed to render a verdict. The verdict is final, and the arbitrator gives an award or gives a decision to the interested parties.

On the first day of the hearing, the DeBarberies and Sline offered their explanations of what had transpired before and during the construction process. The next day, as Marshal sat in the arbitrator's waiting room waiting to testify, the DeBarberies' lawyer, Russell Goodguy, came out of a conference room and handed Marshal a copy of engineering calculations and a report that Sline's engineering expert had prepared and that Goodguy had just received from Sline's lawyer. Looking at the date on the documents, Marshal could see that the engineer had prepared the report several weeks prior to the arbitration date, so Sline's lawyer had waited until the last minute to give the report to Goodguy. Sline's lawyer was obviously trying to limit the amount of time that Marshal could review the report without being able to consult his books and technical journals in his office.

In a normal trial, experts exchange engineering reports and calculations well in advance so that each expert can evaluate the opposing expert's position. The same rules do not apply in arbitration hearings; however, within the five minutes that had been allotted for Marshal to review the opposing engineer's report and calculations, he was able to discern numerous mistakes in logic and application of scientific engineering principles to which he could testify. The sequential license number of the engineer's seal told Marshal that the engineer had recently become licensed, indicating to Marshal that the engineer probably had minimal practical engineering experience in the subject in which he had been hired to offer an opinion.

The arbitrator came out to the lobby and introduced himself as Fred Logan. He asked, "Are you ready?" Marshal then entered the small conference room, introduced himself to the people seated around the conference table, and was offered a seat next to arbitrator Logan. Sitting across from Marshal was Mr. Goodguy. Seated next to Goodguy were Todd and Angela DeBarberie. Howard Erickson sat in his wheelchair at the far end of the table, and as Marshal sat down, Angela reached over to hold Howard's hand. Sitting next to Marshal was Sline's attorney, George Recker, and seated beyond Recker were Randolph Sline and the insurance adjuster representing Sline's construction company.

The hearing proceeded with Marshal explaining the various scientific points derived from each of his observations and tests at the site. The arbitrator asked most of the questions, and because he was sitting immediately adjacent to Marshal, Marshal was able to hand him various photographs and pages from his reports. Marshal could also explain the discrepancies he found in the opposing engineer's report and calculations. Goodguy asked Marshal a few questions, and then it was Mr. Recker's turn to ask him questions.

Marshal turned his chair so that he could face Recker directly. Recker was about the same height as Marshal, and sitting there, Marshal was able to look into Recker's eyes from a distance of about three feet. Unlike other people Marshal had met in life with deep brown eyes, Recker's eyes were dark and sinister. Marshal had seen those eyes on others who had proven themselves capable of evil deeds.

Recker's questioning took Marshal through various points of differences between his observations and opinions as compared to Sline's opposing expert's opinions. During the questioning, Marshal was able to point out that the opposing expert had not even visited the site before rendering his opinion. Finally Recker asked Marshal one last question.

"Have you ever been disciplined by the Texas Board of Professional Engineers?" inquired Recker.

The obvious answer was "no." Marshal knew that he had never been disciplined in Texas or any other state in which he was licensed as a professional engineer.

Then Recker handed Marshal a document and asked him, "Then how do you explain this?"

Marshal read the document silently. At the top of the document it read "Enforcement Detail Report," followed by a case number and "Subject: Yeager, M." The Complainant was Dick Fuelem, P.E. The file had been opened on January 14, 2005, and closed on January 27, 2005. Under "Categories," it read "Residential Foundation—Repair." Under "Comments," it read:

> Mr. Fuelem has filed a complaint against Mr. Yeager alleging that Mr. Yeager makes grandiose, broad, and sweeping statements condemning foundations and frames for houses with little or no supporting codes to support his claims in his reports . . . It was determined that Mr. Yeager provided little information in his reports to support his opinions . . . Mr. Yeager was issued a warning that in the future he should limit his comments to the facts of the specific case in point and provide detailed information, calculations, and/or specific code citations to support his opinions and recommendations.

Marshal had never seen the document before, and in four decades of engineering practice had never heard of an "Enforcement Detail Report." On quick glance, he could see that there was no State of Texas letterhead anywhere on the document and no reference to the Texas Board of Professional Engineers. There was no proven violation shown, nor any citation of any noncompliance with any of the laws or rules governing professional engineers. There was no name identifying the person who had written the words, and there was no signature. As best Marshal could tell, the document was a fake.

Marshal looked at Mr. Goodguy, who by that time had stood up from his chair and said, "Conference outside." Both lawyers and the arbitrator then left the room, taking the document with them. Marshal looked at the DeBarberies and Howard Erickson. There was a look of despair on their faces. Marshal looked at Sline and the insurance adjuster. They were both smiling.

After two minutes, the lawyers and arbitrator Logan returned to the room. Logan said, "I have not read the document and will not offer it into evidence, but you need to answer Mr. Recker's question."

Marshal responded by saying that he was unaware of the facts surrounding the document, but that he did recall that some time in 2004, Mr. Fuelem had cornered one of his female clients alone in a room and had verbally assaulted her. Marshal stated that he did file a complaint against Fuelem as a result of his actions, and Marshal recalled that Fuelem had retaliated by filing a complaint against him. But Marshal had never been questioned by a Board investigator, and to the best of his knowledge there had been no finding against him.

Logan asked, "Did that issue have anything to do with concrete foundations?" Marshal recalled that at the time, he had been testifying against one of Fuelem's foundation assessments. Marshal answered "yes" to the question.

Even though Marshal had done exhaustive work on the case being heard that day by the arbitrator—as he had done in his other forensic investigations over the past decades including providing detailed information, calculations, and specific code citations to support opinions and recommendations—the mere existence of the document combined with Marshal's "yes" answer to the question were all that the arbitrator needed.

Two days later, the arbitrator announced his decision to the lawyers. Mr. Goodguy then telephoned Angela and gave her the news. The arbitrator had decided that the DeBarberies were to receive nothing other than a release of Sline's lien on their property. The money that Angela had received from selling her parents' house was gone.

Howard Erickson grew deeply despondent while watching his daughter's reaction to the news. Howard realized only then that Angela and Todd were financially ruined. With Howard's own wife having died only the year before, he cried silently all that night, grieving alone in the living room while listening to his daughter cry in her bedroom. Then the next morning, while sitting in his wheelchair at the breakfast table, Howard suddenly died. His simple efforts at life, liberty, and pursuit of happiness were gone forever.

It would be much later that Marshal would learn that the DeBarberies were about to enter bankruptcy, but Marshal learned about Howard's death almost immediately. Angela telephoned Marshal in hysterics, first pointing the finger of blame for her father's death directly at Marshal and then apologizing to Marshal for her overreaction. Normally Marshal had solid control of his emotions, but in this instance Marshal was so angry at what had happened to the DeBarberie family that he almost lost his own sense of self-control. He tried to comfort Angela over the phone, but Todd was there and Marshal listened as he heard Todd plead with her to hang up the phone. Then Marshal heard a simple click in his ear as Angela hung up.

Marshal knew that it is against the law to present, or cause to be presented, a false document in a legal setting that results in a decision in which one party gains a superior advantage over another for financial gain. He also knew that it is a crime to manipulate or tamper with a witness. In addition, if a conspirator deliberately sets in motion a chain of events that he knows will cause a third party to commit an illegal act, the conspirator is criminally responsible for that act. If that act results in the death of a person, then the criminal charge could potentially be negligent homicide or even murder.

Marshal now recognized that there were forces at work to discredit him and ruin people's lives for ill-gotten financial gains. After a few moments, Marshal decided what he would do. He would find the person or persons behind the heinous crimes and bring them to justice.

10

ೆ A FOUNDATION OF KNOWLEDGE ೨

For a week, Marshal made telephone calls to friends, clients, and other engineers who might be able to provide insight as to the person or persons responsible for the fraudulent document that Sline's lawyer, Recker, had produced at the arbitration hearing. Recker had put the document in his briefcase after Marshal answered his questions, and because the arbitrator had refused to enter the document into evidence, Marshal had no way to obtain the document from the arbitrator or anybody else. It was quite certain that Recker would not voluntarily turn the document over to Marshal.

After Marshal had returned to the office following the hearing, he had immediately sent a letter to a director of the Texas Board of Professional Engineers asking if the Board was the source of the defamatory information but had not yet received a reply. He had also telephoned a clerk at the Board, asking if anyone with the agency had sent anything about him to Recker or Sline, but the clerk had stated that no such request had been made by anyone of either name.

Marshal recalled that Dick Fuelem, P.E., the engineer listed on the document, was the same engineer who Marshal had previously caught conspiring with another engineer to enter a fraudulent document into a city record in Round Rock, Texas. That incident had occurred the summer just before the beginning of the trial involving Sandra Bullock and her homebuilder. Then it was several weeks later when Fuelem had verbally assaulted Marshal's client.

Marshal knew that Fuelem worked for Joe Tuel, P.E., and that Tuel's engineering firm, Tuel Foundation Engineering or TFE, had been heavily involved for many years in the design of house concrete foundations for homebuilders. TFE specialized in the type of residential concrete foundations that utilized stressed steel cables.

Marshal telephoned the civil engineering department at the University of Texas to see if any of the professors there might be aware of Joe Tuel's involvement with stressed steel cable foundations. The department receptionist gave him the name of several civil engineering professors, one of whom was Bill Kamaka, PhD. Marshal instantly recognized the name of his friend whom he had not seen in several decades.

Marshal then telephoned Bill. The two old friends caught up on the phone awhile and then Marshal asked him if he knew anything about Joe Tuel. Bill told Marshal that he vaguely recalled the name and had heard another professor mention him, so he might be able to help. Bill and Marshal agreed to meet the next day.

At the appointed time, Marshal arrived on the fourth floor of Cockrell Hall at the University of Texas's Cockrell School of Engineering. He finally located Bill's office. As he read the plaque on the wall next to the open door, he felt pride for his friend. *Who would have ever though that Bill could make it so far*, he thought to himself. The plaque read "Professor William (Bill) Kamaka, PhD—Department of Civil Engineering." Marshal knocked loudly on the door jamb, looking past the open door into the office.

Professor Bill Kamaka was sitting in a chair behind his cluttered desk reading a book, facing away from the door. Bill spun around in his chair, jumped to his feet and, smiled broadly as he said, "Hello, Marshal, long time no see. Come on in."

Bill Kamaka was a hulking man. He had dark skin, was of mixed Hawaiian and African ancestry, and was well over six feet tall. Bill was wearing beige slacks and an open-collar white shirt and loosened tie. Marshal saw that Bill was much heavier than he had been when he and Marshal worked together in Houston in the 1960s. In Bill's youth, he had played football while attending one of the then-segregated high schools in Houston. He had not been able to qualify for an athletic scholarship to help pay his way through college, but he was able to qualify for an academic scholarship to Texas A&I University. There he had graduated with a bachelor's degree in civil engineering. After graduation, both he and Marshal met for the first time at Green and Arbor, the large Houston construction and engineering firm.

Because racial segregation still existed in Texas in the 1960s and Marshal was a white man with an advanced degree, the Green and Arbor management had assigned Marshal the responsibility of supervising Bill Kamaka's work performance. The management also assigned Marshal to supervise another engineer who had Asian ancestry, George Yip. The three-man team became the first minority-comprised engineering team at Green and Arbor in the firm's history. Now over 30 years later, Marshal and his old colleague shared a friendly handshake.

"It's good to see you again, Bill. You've really done well for yourself."

Bill walked over and closed the door to his office. "Marshal, we can catch up later but time is short, and I wanted to tell you what I found after you called me." Both men then sat down.

"You told me about what happened at your client's arbitration hearing," Bill began. "You also told me that this guy, what's his name . . . Fuelem . . . worked for Tuel Foundation Engineering out of Dallas and San Antonio. You also told me that you had already had a few encounters with the head of TFE—Joe Tuel."

"That's right, Bill," Marshal said. "I caught Joe Tuel trying to force a bad foundation engineering repair design onto one of my clients. I alerted the city of what he was trying to do, and the city shut the project down. Then Tuel filed a complaint against me with the Texas Board of Professional Engineers, and I got a threatening letter from the agency staff warning me to back off TFE and not to say anything bad about them. I was curious at the time why a state government agency would be protecting a private engineering corporation by issuing a warning to me, but I didn't have the time to follow up on it."

"Marshal, I don't remember meeting Joe Tuel," Bill said, "but his name was vaguely familiar to me so I called someone I know, Dr. Roger Vlasov Fiskman, who is a professor of engineering at Texas

A&M. Dr. Fiskman told me that he was Joe Tuel's partner back in the early 1970s. Joe Tuel graduated from Texas A&M in the 1960s. Dr. Fiskman and Joe Tuel wrote a paper together about the effects of expansive soils on concrete pavements, the same type of methodology that is used today to design tensioned steel cable concrete foundations for houses."

"I remember that paper," Marshal said. "In fact, I had moved back to Austin by that time, and my employer assigned me the task of creating a computer program to facilitate the design of a uniquely reinforced concrete slab on ground foundation system for a large apartment project to be built on expansive clay soils in Austin. I thought at the time that that particular paper that you mentioned was rather weak for a practical purpose, so I designed the foundation system in accordance with a government-issued standard that called for conventional rebar 'mat steel' in the slabs and also conventional rebar in the concrete turn-down grade beams of the foundation. I also included tensioned steel cable technology commonly employed within the structural concrete floor systems of parking garages. I remember that I had just recently designed a parking garage in Austin. By combining both types of steel reinforcing systems—conventional rebar as well as stressed steel cables—I was able to produce a unique foundation design that was usable for house and apartment foundations on expansive clay soils. The project was built and exhibited no foundation deficiencies throughout its lifetime."

"You probably did not know this," said Bill, "but both Dr. Fiskman and I sat together on the same research committee in 1975 that tried to establish engineering design procedures for tensioned steel cable concrete foundations for residential structures because no established procedures existed at that time. As you know, most houses in the southern and far western United States do not have basements, and there was a hope that houses could be built with foundations at lower cost by utilizing both rebar and tensioned steel cables together. The committee then disbanded in dissent over its failure to find a way to make the foundations less expensive, because some of the members wanted to eliminate most if not all of the conventional rebar steel and substitute the steel cables. Also a series of technical articles by other researchers had already offered contradictory results to those obtained by Joe Tuel and Dr. Fiskman.

"Now here is where things became dicey. Dr. Fiskman returned to Texas A&M University, and the university was approached by the Wire Cable Tensioning Institute, commonly called WCTI, which is a trade organization that sells steel cables worldwide. They provided a grant to Texas A&M University in the late 1970s so that Dr. Fiskman could develop a procedure that would enable structural engineers to design residential concrete foundations incorporating their tensioned steel cable product while remaining competitive with the conventional foundation systems using rebar that were designed by engineers of that day.

"Because the real purpose for WCTI paying for the research was to find a way to sell as many steel cables as possible, Dr. Fiskman and some of his engineering students then devised computational solutions that would maximize the amount of steel tendons that would be installed in concrete foundations and minimize the amount of conventional reinforcing steel. We're talking about tons of steel cable here and billions of dollars for the members of WCTI. Full-size testing of actual concrete foundations either wasn't done or wasn't reported. With all factors considered, the system developed by Dr. Fiskman and his students turned out to be more expensive than the old methodology of designing foundation systems using conventional rebar.

"What happened next," Bill continued, "has become a topic of much dispute among researchers. According to Dr. Fiskman, the WCTI was not pleased with his results because his research did not prove that the costs of foundations that utilized the stressed cable concept would be lower. In fact, the costs would be higher when the cables are combined with conventional mat steel rebar. Dr. Fiskman's efforts turned out to be a waste of time because the best foundation systems that engineers could design were the ones that engineers had been designing all along using only conventional rebar and no cables. The WCTI paid A&M for Dr. Fiskman's research, as they had previously agreed to do. But then as the story goes, in a deliberate plan to make the house foundations cheaper while using stressed steel cables, WCTI eliminated the entire chapter from Dr. Fiskman's research report that had called for the inclusion of conventional mat steel, the same type of mat steel rebar that you, Marshal, had evidently incorporated into your design back in the early 1970s. They also eliminated some of the concrete, just enough to make the ultimate house foundations cheaper than they would be if they were properly designed foundations containing rebar. They made house foundations less expensive all right, but they also made them much more flexible, weaker, and prone to moving and cracking, causing many of the problems that you see today with concrete foundations on expansive soils. Then in 1980, WCTI published a slick paper guide on the procedure and sent it to practically every structural engineer in Texas and maybe the nation. They even gave the impression that Dr. Fiskman had authored the guide."

"Then you're telling me," Marshal sputtered, "that since 1980, the WCTI organization has deliberately omitted a significant portion of Dr. Fiskman's work in order to sell more steel cables, and has also been aware of the fact that their steel cable concrete foundations would fail? And the system has not even been tested by Dr. Fiskman using actual slabs? Why didn't Dr. Fiskman blow the whistle on them?"

"The WCTI lawyers had a firm confidentiality clause in their contract with Texas A&M," Bill replied. "No one at A&M was allowed to talk about it. Not even Dr. Roger Fiskman himself. Otherwise, the university and Dr. Fiskman would get sued. I guess you are not aware that much of the corporate money that goes into university research nowadays has many strings attached. Those strings are attached in a way that many professors and other researchers are not allowed to disclose actual test results that could show that the product, like a concrete foundation, is not all it's cracked up to be. Please pardon my bad pun. By the way, do you know June Melton, P.E.? He had a similar problem arranging for money for university research on the connections for pre-engineered wood trusses, and he said he learned that researchers were not being allowed to disclose the full extent of their testing."

"I don't know him," Marshal said.

"He's semiretired, I think," said Bill, "but still practicing some engineering in Texas and Oklahoma and also writing books out in Coronado, California. But Marshal, after talking to Dr. Fiskman there are probably many members of the homebuilding industry that do know what is going on with these WCTI foundation systems, particularly the large multistate homebuilders. However, I believe that there are some smaller homebuilders who don't know what is going on. All of the builders are looking for the cheapest foundation system they can get their engineers to design.

"There's another engineering professor here who told me that some of his students, along with some of Charles Berrenchino's employees, tested a bunch of full-size house foundations. They found that the foundations failed, and the WCTI methodology was no good. Do you know Charles Berrenchino? He's a local engineering consultant."

"Yes, I do know who Charles is," Marshal said. "In fact, I worked with him on several engineering projects for a short time. And he did tell me about those tests. That's one reason why for years I've been warning other engineers and clients to avoid using the WCTI method. I asked him why the group's findings had not been published, and Charles said that someone associated with the WCTI research program had come by his office and asked for the original copies but never returned them. He said that when he contacted that person again, the guy denied ever going to Charles's office. Charles did not give me the name of that person. So I continued to design residential foundations the way I always had before the WCTI method was published, using conventional rebar and leaving out the steel cables altogether. Sure my designs were somewhat more expensive than those using the WCTI methods, but my foundations did not move or structurally crack even when installed in expansive clay soils."

"Marshal," Bill said, "if the WCTI recognized that their foundations would fail in 1980, then how do you think they have been able to keep this under wraps for so many years?"

"By trying to force acceptance of their WCTI standards onto the engineers who design residential foundations," Marshal replied. "The procedure never went through proper academic peer review at the engineering universities. In 1993, President Bill Clinton signed the NAFTA treaty, and then there began an influx of large homebuilding corporations into Texas. I began to detect politics or lobbying at the Texas Board of Professional Engineers. It appeared to me at the time that the WCTI may have been putting pressure on members of the Board."

"What makes you think that?" Bill asked.

"The Board issued a warning to all professional engineers in the state in one of its newsletters," Marshal said. "The Board announced that it would be adopting or endorsing the WCTI design method as a mandatory method for design engineers to follow when designing residential concrete foundations. I personally attended the Board meeting and advised the Board members of what I had learned about the WCTI procedure, specifically the fact that the procedure had not been openly tested by its proponents. I urged the Board to not allow WCTI to monopolize the residential foundation construction trade with their steel cables, because a group of professional engineers including myself were becoming convinced that the WCTI system did not work. We did not want to design foundations utilizing the design methodology. The Board accepted my advice at the time.

"Homebuyer lawsuits began in earnest in the 1990s. Many structural engineers who designed residential foundations for builders that utilized the WCTI method quickly found that their builder-clients were angry at the engineers, because the homebuying customers were angry at the builders. The builders had no practical way to repair the defective foundations that their engineers had designed. Homebuyers were complaining about walls and ceilings cracking, doors jamming that could not be opened or closed, and roof rafters buckling soon after the homebuyers had moved into the houses. Many engineers either learned to risk a builder's lawsuit or stopped designing tensioned cable residential foundations altogether.

"Meanwhile," Marshal continued, "homebuilders grew accustomed to constructing the inexpensive foundations. Hundreds of thousands of concrete foundations were designed by engineers utilizing the WCTI procedure in Texas. The large homebuilding corporations used them almost exclusively because they could save an average of $3,000 per house on the foundation, which results in a savings of about $30 per month on a homebuyer's mortgage. The builders could also easily afford to defend themselves in court against any homeowner-brought lawsuits.

"In a normal year, homebuilders build over 100,000 new homes per year in Texas. If only one large homebuilding corporation built two thousand houses a year, it could expect to save about 6 million dollars per year on foundations alone and then use that capital to expand to other states like California, Nevada, and Florida. Meanwhile, the smaller homebuilders were faced with a choice of trying to compete by installing the less-expensive WCTI foundations; or construct proper foundations designed by engineers like me and face the prospect of less profit per house or of overpricing the local market.

"As I alluded to earlier, it was in the early 1990s when I first began to suspect that the WCTI group may have been lobbying the Texas Board of Professional Engineers to force engineers to employ steel cables in their foundation designs. But by 1999, I began to suspect that an alliance was forming between the WCTI, the steel cable corporations, and the homebuilders to actually try to corrupt the Texas Board of Professional Engineers."

At that moment, there was a knock on Bill's office door. Bill said, "That's probably my daughter, Brooke. Maybe she can tell us what's going on at the Board. She works there."

11

❧ THE FUELEM CONFESSION ❧

Bill Kamaka walked to the door and opened it for his youngest daughter. "Come on in, Brooke. I want to introduce you to an old friend of mine, Marshal Yeager." Marshal stood up and greeted the young woman.

Brooke Kamaka was an attractive, dark-skinned brunette, about 28-years-old, medium height, and wore a gray business suit. She also wore businesslike glasses that seemed to emphasize the fact that she was intelligent and professional. She carried a black briefcase in her left hand and held out her right hand. Marshal shook her hand.

Bill had mentioned Brooke to Marshal on the phone. Brooke was born long after Marshal had left Houston. As a child she had been an excellent student and continued to make high grades at Houston's Bellaire High School. As happens to many teenagers, Brooke had befriended some students who did not share her happy background and were troublemakers. Those friends had elicited Brooke's sympathy.

Bill and his wife, Michelle, had given Brooke a car for her birthday, and Brooke had unwittingly loaned the car to her friends. The friends not only wrecked her car but at the same time were being chased by the Houston police for shoplifting. After that, Brooke decided that whatever others did in life was up to them. She was going to think about her own future and live her own life as a free, intelligent individual who was not going to get dragged down by other people's problems.

After graduating from Bellaire, Brooke then enrolled at the University of Texas. She became active in campus life, maintained a high grade point average, and was elected for membership in the Tau Beta Pi engineering honor society. She graduated with her bachelor of science degree in environmental engineering and went on to work for the Department of Defense in Washington. She subsequently decided to return to the University of Texas to get her master's degree in civil engineering and possibly her doctorate later.

Bill, Marshal, and Brooke found their chairs and sat down. "Marshal," Bill said, "I've asked Brooke to meet with us today because she might be able to help you find the source of that fraudulent document that showed up at the arbitration hearing."

"That's right, Mr. Yeager," Brooke said. "Dad asked me to help you because I work at the Texas Board of Professional Engineers. He told me what happened to you and your clients at that arbitration hearing."

"Brooke, first off, please call me Marshal. Tell me, are you here in an official capacity?"

She smiled. "No, Marshal. I'm here as a spy. I work there part time."

Marshal grinned. "What kind of spy are you?" he asked.

"One who can't stand to be around people who take advantage of others and who break the law. There are actually a lot of young people who do what I do. No disrespect intended, Marshal, but your generation has pretty well messed up my generation's future and our constitutional liberties, and it will take my generation an entire lifetime for this country to pay off the irresponsible debt and interest on that debt that the government of your generation now owes to other countries, especially China. I worked for a short time at the Department of Defense. As you may know, after 9/11 the Federal Bureau of Investigation asked all engineers to report instances of fraud and corruption that they witness to the FBI for investigation because building and housing construction involves a great deal of money changing hands. Based on a tip, I was asked to take a job at the Texas

Board of Professional Engineers, and while working there I can still work on my master's. The law enforcement authorities regard engineers as insightful, resourceful, logical, detail-oriented, and patriotic. Others like me are working underground inside other federal and state agencies to help catch the so-called enemies within—those who profit at the expense of the American people."

"Brooke," Bill said, "before you came in just now, I told Marshal that I had spoken with Dr. Fiskman at Texas A&M, who confirmed that the WCTI altered his research on stressed cable house foundations. I mentioned Dr. Fiskman and Joe Tuel to you and another fellow named Dick Fuelem, whose name Marshal said appeared on the fraudulent document. Dick Fuelem works for Joe Tuel. I told Marshal that Dr. Fiskman and Joe Tuel had worked together on a paper, and Marshal told me that he had grown concerned that some kind of alliance may have been formed between the WCTI steel cable corporations and the homebuilding industry to corrupt the Texas Board of Professional Engineers. Correct me if I am wrong here, Marshal, but you implied that the purpose of the alliance was to force all the engineers in Texas who design residential foundations to use steel cables in their foundations and not other, better systems with conventional rebar. If the Texas Board of Professional Engineers is really in alliance with those people, then that would mean that the State of Texas is trying to force a monopoly onto the homebuying consumer as well as the engineers."

"That is something," Marshal said, "that I really believe began to occur in the early to mid-1990s. By 1999, the WCTI standards were under attack by professional engineers throughout the state. I attended a symposium held in Houston and hundreds of structural engineers attended from across the nation. We learned that a staff member of the Texas Board of Professional Engineers had been meeting privately with WCTI advocates, and he had resigned from his state employment shortly before the symposium. Joe Tuel, your friend Dr. Roger Fiskman, and three other developers or users of the WCTI method spoke to the engineers at that symposium using favorable terms. However, by the time the symposium was over, all of the engineers in the room that I talked to were swearing they would never use the method again to design any residential foundations. I got a distinct impression during that symposium that Tuel and Fiskman had entered into some kind of partnership."

"Let me interject something here," Brooke said. "Before I came here today, I did research on the period of time you were just talking about. I learned that a staff member of the Texas Board of Professional Engineers had been meeting privately with members of the Alpine Residential Foundation Design Association, which is a group of engineers who are WCTI advocates and who design foundations for homebuilders. The purpose of those meetings was to get the Texas Board of Professional Engineers to establish public policy that would require all structural engineers in Texas to utilize the WCTI standards and prohibit other methods of design, which would certainly benefit the steel cable and homebuilding industries. Also, they all agreed that engineers who spoke irreverently about WCTI standards would be disciplined by the Board for what they said or wrote. The Texas Board of Professional Engineers intended to regulate engineers by requiring them to 'communicate using clear and concise language.' The question there was how does the state objectively regulate language that is 'clear and concise' without violating an engineer's First Amendment rights? The Board staff withdrew the proposed rules right before that symposium in Houston you spoke about in 1999 because they were getting an earful from professional engineers in private practice. But you should be able to see the drift that the Board was starting to take.

"The proposal to effectively suspend the First Amendment rights of professional engineers did not die right there," continued Brooke. "It went underground, cloistered in the offices of the Texas Board of Professional Engineers. After Governor Rick Perry came into power, he placed at least one WCTI engineer-advocate on the Board. Also now when there is a complaint filed against any of the WCTI engineers, the Board staff either delays investigating for a long time, or quickly dismisses the complaints. They are considered to be 'protected engineers.'"

"Brooke," Marshal said, "do you know if Joe Tuel or Dick Fuelem sat on any of the committees involving the Alpine group or have any linkage to the Texas Board of Professional Engineers?"

"Joe Tuel was involved at the committee level," answered Brooke, "but I don't know that Dick Fuelem was because I have not researched his name on anything other than the arbitration matter directly associated with you."

"After that Houston symposium," Marshal said, "the City of San Antonio housing authority issued a request for qualifications for design and construction of a large public-housing project consisting of over 200 single-family homes. The housing authority required the professional engineers to design only conventional rebar foundations for the homes, the same as I had been doing for decades. They shut out the WCTI procedure completely by saying something like 'tensioned-steel slabs not acceptable, conventional reinforcing only.' That action represented a significant blow to the steel cable industry that has been evidently trying to monopolize the market for more than a decade. About that time, the City of Austin also mandated that all sites must be designed by a structural engineer in accordance with recognized engineering design criteria. Then after that symposium, with most of the engineers getting out of the business of designing residential foundations, Joe Tuel and his foundation firm, TFE, began to dominate the engineered foundation design market. They designed tens of thousands of tensioned steel cable concrete foundations for large nationwide corporate homebuilders. Very few of the other engineers wanted anything to do with it.

"Tuel also became an expert witness working on behalf of homebuilders that were being sued by homeowners. I didn't know very much about Joe Tuel until the early 2000s. He and I became opposing experts in many disputes brought by homebuyers against homebuilders. Tuel seems to have become an expert in demand by the homebuilders. He once told me that he had testified in almost 200 cases, almost all of which were on behalf of homebuilders.

"Then other engineering firms entered the residential foundation design market, not suspecting that the foundations they were designing using the WCTI method did not adequately resist the movement caused by expansive clay soils. Those engineers had apparently not attended the Houston symposium or mistakenly thought the procedure might work. Also, about that time builders began to include binding arbitration into their non-negotiable sales contracts. The houses would move and crack, the homebuyer would be forced into binding arbitration by the builder, and Tuel would testify in defense of the builder, saying that the builder's structural engineer had correctly followed the standards, and there was nothing wrong with the house.

"It was in the early 2000s when I really began to suspect that something was really wrong with Tuel and TFE and that there might be some kind of covert arrangement underway between Tuel, WCTI, the homebuilders, insurance corporations, and the Texas Board of Professional Engineers. On one hand, Tuel would testify in defense of a homebuilder, saying that the builder's structural engineer had correctly followed the standards, and there was nothing wrong with the house. Then later, whenever the builder wanted to file suit against his own foundation design engineer for any losses sustained by the builder, Tuel would testify that the foundation engineer had correctly followed the standards but had misinterpreted the soil properties. Therefore the claim against the engineer would be covered by the engineer's liability insurance carrier. In the end, the builder could recover his losses to the homeowner by receiving his money back from the engineer's insurance carrier. The liability insurance companies then raised the insurance premiums paid by all professional engineers and fattened their own profits. In turn, the engineers raised their fees for designing the foundations, and the homebuilders correspondingly increased the prices of their houses for sale."

"Marshal," Brooke said, "I can say that the engineer-made-a-mistake argument is being made at the Texas Board of Professional Engineers even now. The Board's position is evidently the same as Mr. Tuel's, which is that the standards are not to be questioned; so the reason the house had moved and was cracking was because the engineer had misinterpreted the soil characteristics or misapplied the WCTI standards. Several engineers have been disciplined by the Board under that premise."

"Marshal," Bill said, "I know that the Texas Board of Professional Engineers has asked for engineers outside the agency to testify in technical matters against engineers disciplined by the Board. I know because they have asked me to volunteer. If Tuel is such a so-called expert in demand as you indicate, do you think he is testifying against the engineers being disciplined?"

"Bill, I can't say for sure," replied Marshal. "I think it is some kind of secret tribunal where there is only one outside engineer who offers an opinion to the Board staff. Wait . . . do you think that tribunal engineer might be Joe Tuel?"

"It's possible," said Bill. "You said a moment ago that you had previous problems with Tuel and that the Board staff had told you to back off criticizing him and TFE. It sounds to me that Tuel might have some kind of inside connection with the state agency."

"I can tell you that he is one of the protected engineers," said Brooke, "but I don't know if he is this tribunal engineer you describe."

"Well," said Marshal, "one favorable thing I have said in the past about Tuel and TFE is that over an extended period of time, I have noticed that very few of the residential foundations designed by TFE had cracked, moved, or otherwise failed. So in that regard, I thought they were providing a proper engineering design service. However, I had also suspected that TFE might not only have driven out the competition for designing residential foundations and hiked its fees to the homebuilders, but TFE may have been secretly beefing up its own designs over what the WCTI standards required, including calling for mat reinforcing steel in the slab portions of the foundations as I had done in the early 1970s. I began to suspect that the homebuilders were paying for more expensive foundations and didn't even know it. Then one day, quite by chance, my suspicions were confirmed. Bill, you remember I gave you Dick Fuelem's name when I called you about that fraudulent document produced at the arbitration?"

"Yes, you gave me his name, and I gave it to Brooke. But otherwise I had not heard of him before you called me," Bill said.

"Well, I've learned a lot about him," Marshal said. "He's a structural engineer who runs the San Antonio office of TFE. One day toward the end of 2003, I went to the TFE offices to pick up a file a client had asked me to get. While waiting for the file, I sat in the office kitchen sipping hot tea when Fuelem walked in to get some coffee. I had met Fuelem only once before, during a conference at another office. He seemed polite, so I asked him to sit down and join me while I waited for the clerk to bring me the file. He grabbed a cup of coffee and sat down across the table from me.

"I asked him about various aspects of his career. I asked him if he was happy working for TFE, running the San Antonio office while being directed by Joe Tuel up in Dallas. Was he happy with his career as a professional engineer? Was he happy designing foundations using the WCTI design method? Fuelem had answered 'no' to all of my questions.

"I then decided to expand my questioning and asked him what the other engineers at TFE thought about the WCTI method. Fuelem answered, 'We stopped believing years ago that the system works. We've been beefing up our designs, adding extra concrete and steel.'"

"Wait, what did you say?" interrupted Bill. "Let me get this straight. Did Fuelem actually confess to you that the engineers at TFE were beefing up their designs for their builder-clients because they knew that the WCTI standards were bad?"

"I almost gasped myself when I heard Fuelem's answer," Marshal replied. "The answer is yes. Fuelem actually confessed that the TFE engineers knew that the standards were bad, apparently not realizing that I already knew that Tuel was saying in court that the standards were good. Then when I asked Fuelem if Joe Tuel agreed with him that the WCTI standards were bad, Fuelem's face turned deathly white. He couldn't open his mouth to answer the question. I suspect that Tuel had previously warned Fuelem not to talk to me, but Fuelem had already let the cat out of the bag, and he knew it. Then the file clerk entered the kitchen and handed me the file that I had come for. I said goodbye to Fuelem and left the TFE office."

12

CG CHICAGO-STYLE TORT REFORM ഌ

"**B**rooke," said Marshal, "before you came in, Bill and I had already discussed the fact that Joe Tuel and Dr. Roger Fiskman had written a paper together concerning concrete slabs on expansive soils and that the two of them had spoken favorably about the WCTI method at the Houston symposium. Now, Dr. Fiskman has admitted to Bill that WCTI altered the research that Dr. Fiskman did on stressed cable house foundations.

"We have Joe Tuel, the head of TFE, who was possibly more than just a coauthor with Dr. Fiskman on a technical paper. Tuel is possibly in an actual partnership with Dr. Fiskman. TFE now dominates the concrete slab foundation market in Texas, designing hundreds of thousands of tensioned steel cable concrete foundations for large nationwide corporate homebuilders. I have been convinced for some time now that TFE has been adding more materials to their designs so that their foundations would not move and crack, like the ones that other engineers design using strictly WCTI standards. But doing it that way increases the overall cost of a foundation system, greater than it would be if they had simply left the steel cables out and used regular rebar reinforcing. Also, whenever one of Tuel's homebuilder-clients gets sued by a homeowner, Tuel steps in as an expert witness for the builder and testifies that nothing is wrong. But in a small number of instances when a homebuilder uses another engineering firm to design the foundations and the homebuyer files suit against the homebuilder,

Tuel steps in as an expert witness to testify that the standards are good and that it was the foundation engineer who made a mistake. Or if the home is located in the same subdivision and founded on the same types of soils as one of Tuel's builder-clients, I have seen him testify that the standards are good and the foundation engineer did *not* make a mistake. Tuel might also be a protected engineer at the Texas Board of Professional Engineers, and Tuel and some staff members of the agency potentially maintain direct or indirect connections to the Alpine Residential Design Association as well as WCTI. What a bunch of interlocking relationships!

"Then there is Dick Fuelem who admitted to me that the TFE engineers knew that the standards didn't work, and he admitted that they were beefing up their designs by adding extra concrete and steel. Judging from Fuelem's reaction to my question as to whether or not Joe Tuel felt the same way as Fuelem did about the WCTI method, undoubtedly Fuelem got with Tuel later and told him that I now know that the entire WCTI method is a scam. Tuel's entire livelihood as an expert witness depends on a perpetuation of that scam.

"In addition, we have a staff member of the Texas Board of Professional Engineers meeting privately with some engineers who are WCTI advocates and who design foundations for homebuilders. They also are encouraging the Texas Board of Professional Engineers to allow WCTI to monopolize the procedure for the design of residential concrete foundations in Texas in order to benefit the steel cable and homebuilding industries in the state.

"Next we have the City of San Antonio that finally decides to shut out the WCTI design procedure completely from its projects and requires engineers to go back to design foundations with conventional rebar only. When a government agency refuses to accept a design standard any longer, then that could also negatively affect Tuel's entire foundation design operation as well as the future of his engineering firm, TFE.

"Then we have the anti–First Amendment WCTI and Alpine group advocates who want the Texas Board of Professional Engineers to restrict an engineer's writings and speech to 'clear and concise language.' That appears to be little more than an overt threat against engineers who offer expert testimony on behalf of homebuyers against homebuilders in court. I doubt that you would ever have any of the WCTI advocates disciplined for speaking incorrectly, but I'll bet that you would have the engineers who testify on behalf of homeowners disciplined for improper speech."

"Marshal, I have several things to add to that topic when you are finished," said Brooke.

"And then now," Marshal continued, "Governor Rick Perry places one, maybe more, of those WCTI advocates on the engineering Board. One thing that I did not mention previously was that I had investigated the Aggie Bonfire collapse reports several years ago, and I still believe that the governor's office might have applied pressure to either to the full Board or to the state staff, or both. The Bonfire matter is still winding its way through the courts as we speak. Also, Governor Perry signed the bill promoted by homebuilders that created the state agency to protect builders from consumers called the Texas Residential Construction Commission. It is now used as a way to either delay a homebuyer's complaint against a builder for years, or to simply dismiss the homebuyer's complaint outright.

"Okay, Brooke," said Marshal. "I'm finished with my little spiel. You go ahead."

"You are correct," said Brooke. "The Texas Board of Professional Engineers has been trying to restrict the speech of professional engineers who testify as expert witnesses on behalf of homebuyers in court and at arbitration. I want to show you some of the documents that I brought with me from the Texas Board of Professional Engineers that affect you personally and professionally. But I want to show you first what they did to another engineer before they started in on you."

"Brooke," said Bill, "does that briefcase have any confidential documents in it that you shouldn't let us see?"

"I don't know about that," she said. "All I know is that a friend at the agency copied them and then told me to take them to whomever I wanted. She also suggested that I take them to the district attorney."

Brooke turned to face Marshal. "Marshal, I first heard your name mentioned at the agency offices about a year ago, and I recognized your name because my Dad has always spoken about you. A lawyer using the Texas Open Records Act recently contacted one of the people in the Records department and asked that records be pulled on several engineers. I work in Records so I went to the files and discovered that your records had been pulled by that same lawyer several years ago. I didn't like what the documents said about you and the other engineers, so I asked my supervisor about them. That's when she copied the records and handed them to me. Most of the records are supposed to be destroyed within three years, but in your case they had slipped up or somebody deliberately decided not to destroy them. I then talked to a friend of mine who is a lawyer. There are bad things going on over there where I work, very dishonest things."

"Wait a second, Brooke," Marshal said. "If a lawyer contacted the agency and had somebody copy my records that far back, then why wasn't I notified? One of the first things I did after that recent arbitration hearing was go to the Board's Web site. It says right there on their site that the Open Records Act requires the agency to make a good faith effort to contact the engineer whenever anyone requests the engineer's records. I know for a fact that I have never received such a notice."

Brooke smiled. "The agency Web site contains false information. My lawyer friend says that the actual statute does not say that they have to inform you if somebody pulls your records. Most lawyers know that, but most engineers don't. The agency posts that notice in order to throw off the engineers. There are lawyers, or engineers who are working for lawyers, who are having engineers' records pulled all the time over there without the engineers finding out until much later, if at all. Marshal, they've even released your scholastic records from UT going back to the 1960s. I've seen them. Not too shabby your junior and senior years, but I won't mention your freshman and sophomore years. Good thing you didn't ever go on scholastic probation because if you testify in court, a lawyer questioning you about that could make it be pretty embarrassing for you. Also they've released your test scores on the professional licensing exam. You passed on the first try. There's no such thing as privacy over there."

"I wonder if they released my medical records from the UT health center as well," Marshal grumbled. "I do remember having a bad case of acne when I was a freshman, so I guess that might come up during a trial, too."

Brooke smiled as she reached into her briefcase and removed various documents. "Okay, Marshal. Now let me start with one of the more blatant cases I found. There's a professional engineer named Meriano. He practices in Dallas doing general structural engineering design and consulting work. He's never had any previous history of complaints filed against him. Then I found a letter that he had written in response to a complaint filed against him. It said he had been working as an expert witness for seven different homeowners, finding defective construction in their houses and testifying against the builders during depositions and trials. His homeowner-clients kept winning their cases.

"Then he mentioned in his letter an engineer named Salven. Salven had been an expert witness working for the homebuilders. Salven's builder-clients kept losing the lawsuits because of Meriano's work. One of the builder's lawyers then filed a lawsuit against Meriano on behalf of Salven claiming that Meriano had slandered Salven during a deposition in one of the defective house cases."

"What happened to the lawsuit against Meriano?" Marshal asked.

"The judge eventually dismissed it, but it probably cost Meriano a lot of money to pay his lawyer to defend against the suit. My lawyer friend said that an expert opinion offered by an engineer in a deposition is privileged testimony and cannot be used against the engineer in court. My friend was surprised that the lawyer who filed the suit would have taken the case in the first place.

"But here is what I think the true motive might be," Brooke continued. "While the lawyer was suing Meriano, behind the scenes the lawyer was evidently trying to get Meriano sanctioned at the Texas Board of Professional Engineers so that he could never testify again. Or if he did testify, then his clients would lose. According to Meriano's letter, Salven's lawyer did not want the judge who was hearing the slander lawsuit to know that the lawyer intended to try to get Meriano's professional engineering license sanctioned by filing a formal complaint with the Board. So instead of filing a formal complaint, he e-mailed some documents with Salven's name and simply described those documents as 'troubling' to a Board staff investigator and his supervisor in Enforcement.

"Somehow, Salven's lawyer must have already known that someone working for the agency would help them get rid of Meriano. The staff Enforcement officer copied the e-mail verbatim, sent a letter to Meriano describing it as a 'staff-initiated complaint,' and enclosed all of the documents they had received by e-mail with no additional information generated by Board staff. The staff Enforcement supervisor wrote that Meriano was being 'misleading and untruthful' and that the Texas Board of Professional Engineers was accepting the complaint on that basis."

"Brooke, what kind of documents did Salven's lawyer e-mail to the Board staff investigator?" Marshal asked.

"Deposition documents. Mr. Meriano discovered deficiencies in a house and gave a deposition in 2003. I've never had to give a deposition, so I don't really know how it works, but my lawyer friend told me that a deposition is a witness's out-of-court testimony that is used as a sworn written statement in court or for discovery purposes. He said that depositions are usually taken in a lawyer's office, and there's a court reporter present to record everything said. My friend told me that expert witnesses are supposed to examine the evidence, conduct research, do calculations, and reach conclusions. If both experts agree in their reports, then the case can be easily resolved. If they disagree, then the differences of opinion are expressed in their reports. But during depositions, the lawyer can ask whatever he or she wants, and the witness is supposed to answer the question. Meriano had been criticizing Salven's work and used three pairs of words that the Board staff said were in violation of the Engineering Practice Act."

"What three pairs of words?" asked Marshal.

"'Recklessly negligent,' 'error ridden,' and 'reckless disregard,'" said Brooke.

"That's ridiculous," Marshal said. "Meriano's an American citizen. Under our constitution, he can use whatever words he wants to describe what he is seeing, especially in a court setting such as a deposition. What happened next, Brooke?"

"In March 2004, Mr. Meriano attended an informal conference at the Board offices. An informal conference is the stage of a complaint after the Board staff has already decided that the engineer is probably guilty of something. The engineer is given the choice to informally plead his or her case, plead guilty and agree to a lesser sanction, or fight the charges and go before an administrative judge where the engineer's license might be suspended or revoked. Almost everyone accused opts for the informal conference.

"According to the record," Brooke continued, "a lawyer from the Texas attorney general's office attended Meriano's informal conference. His name is Paul Corrigan. He was the assistant attorney general who provided legal advice to the Texas Board of Professional Engineers. He advised the Board staff to drop the whole thing because he was concerned that there might be some First Amendment rights involved. At the same time, another lawyer who sits on the Board interceded with the staff's executive director and told her to drop the whole thing for the same reason. That lawyer sits on the Board even now."

"What was the name of the executive director back then?" Marshal asked.

"Back then it would have been Ms. Chinn. I wasn't working for the Texas Board of Professional Engineers back then, but I do remember someone telling me that she quit her job before the summer of 2004. I think it had to do with the pressure she was getting from the governor's office about the A&M Bonfire collapse and the way they wanted the Board to prosecute engineers based on what they say in court."

"So, did the staff drop the complaint against Meriano?" asked Marshal.

"They did for a while," said Brooke, "but in the meantime, the Board tried to get rid of Assistant Attorney General Paul Corrigan. They were eventually successful, but it took them some time. There was some trouble at a Board meeting. As you know, there is the Texas Society of Professional Engineers that works to maintain high standards for professional engineers. The organization makes sure that those engineers enforce the health, safety, and welfare of the general public, and it also advocates for individual engineers who are persecuted by government agencies, hiring lawyers for the engineers if necessary. The Texas Society is part of the National Society of Professional Engineers. Then there is an engineering organization called Engineered Construction for Houston Organizations and Society, or ECHOS, that is less interested in the professionalism of engineering and is more profit-oriented. That group generally consists of engineers who are also contractors—usually roadbuilding contractors or civil engineers who depend on public money for their livelihoods. ECHOS members contribute a lot of money to politicians. They take politicians on junkets and try to curry favor from politicians so that they can get government contracts which, on a federal level, they get through congressional pork-barrel spending or 'earmarks.' They also work at getting state government contracts through various appropriation bills. Also, they are big on Governor Perry's drives for tort reform. One of their missions is to minimize lawsuits any way they can.

"Anyway, Governor Perry appointed at least one advocate for ECHOS to the Board. The lobbyist for the group sat in the audience while that particular Board member tried to get Paul Corrigan replaced with an outside lawyer—someone who is not with the attorney general's office. Paul Corrigan was a state employee, but the Board seemed determined to find a way to make sure that Corrigan and the attorney general's office were kept unaware of what the Texas Board of Professional Engineers was actually up to. The Board and staff can be as reckless as they want to be, and if any legal issues should arise—such as an engineer filing a lawsuit against the Board or staff—the Texas attorney general's office has to represent the Board on behalf of the State of Texas. That was in 2005, and Paul seemed determined to stay. But that didn't stop the staff's efforts to ruin Mr. Meriano."

Brooke handed Marshal a letter with "Texas Board of Professional Engineers" printed across the top and a date of November 2005 directly below. The letter was signed by the staff director of enforcement. Marshal read aloud:

Dear Mr. Meriano:
I have thoroughly reviewed this case and concur with

the investigator that this was not a frivolous case. We also had no basis for determining that the case was filed for the purpose of retaliation. Likewise, as stated in our case-closing letter, you should carefully consider how you characterize your opinions of other professional engineers and their work. A person could potentially be harmed by your use of inflammatory phrases such as 'recklessly negligent,' 'error ridden,' and 'reckless disregard.' For these reasons, this complaint was not deemed frivolous.

"I don't understand," said Marshal. "What are they talking about when they say, 'A person could potentially be harmed by your use of inflammatory phrases.' Are they again criticizing Mr. Meriano about those three word pairs from that 2003 deposition?"

"Yes," said Brooke. "They reopened the case."

"Then what is this agency employee doing using the word 'inflammatory' to describe an engineer's phraseology?" inquired Marshal. "That is about as off the wall as anyone can get. Also, this letter refers to how Meriano characterizes his professional opinions related to the work of other engineers. In this particular case, as you indicated earlier, the work in question is that of a homebuilder's engineer who is serving as an opposing expert in a legal matter. So maybe that gets directly to the heart of what seems to be going on there. The staff is trying to shape the opinions of engineers when they testify in court on behalf of homebuyers, in order to benefit the builders. Brooke, didn't you say that Meriano had successfully testified on numerous occasions on behalf of homebuyers?"

"That's what I said, Marshal. I believe that they are threatening Mr. Meriano as a warning to either stop testifying truthfully for homeowners or face suspension of his professional license. They are threatening expert witnesses who testify on behalf of homeowners."

"It's beginning to look like Governor Perry has found an Al Capone–style method of tort reform," Marshal said. "Tamper with or just rub out the witnesses before they can get to court. This is beginning to look like Chicago gangland politics at work here in Texas.

It's almost like Italian-style fascism. Mussolini would be proud of the concept."

Brooke said, "Let me tell you what I have learned from reading the files. First, if an expert witness has a reputation as a winner for homeowners, then a lawyer working for a homebuilder or an insurance company will have their own expert witness file a complaint against that engineer. Apparently most lawyers don't want to file the complaint themselves because it is too obvious. The complaints are always frivolous—made-up stuff that gives the Board staff an excuse to open an investigation. Usually it is based on something the engineer said or something as silly as not doing equations or arithmetic the same way as the other engineer. Engineers know that no two colleagues perform calculations exactly the same way. Then when the engineer receives a copy of the complaint, the engineer is required to respond, which can take some time and distract the engineer from working on the case and other work. Sometimes the investigator will insist on documents that the engineer cannot yet turn over because the client prohibits it. The staff then drags the process out for several months and then the Board staff closes the file. But depending on whom the engineer is, the staff issues a warning letter or admonishment to the engineer if that particular engineer displeases a construction contractor, homebuilder, or insurance corporation."

Brooke handed Marshal another document. It was a copy of a page from Meriano's deposition. Meriano had answered a question by using the word "perjury." The word had been underlined.

"Well," said Marshal, "after reading this page of Meriano's deposition, if the Board staff is so worried about how engineers express themselves using the English language, then it seems to me that the word 'perjury' would be more inflammatory than the other words he used. Why would the enforcement director not mention Meriano's use of the word 'perjury' in his letter?"

"I asked my lawyer friend the same question," said Brooke. "He thinks the enforcement director did not want to mention it in his letter because perjury is a crime. If an engineer observes or even suspects that a crime has been committed by another engineer, he is obligated to state it in whatever manner he can to the court, through a deposition, and to the authorities if necessary. If the staff becomes aware of a crime, then the staff not only must investigate it but also turn it over to law enforcement authorities. In Meriano's case, the staff did not want law enforcement to know what it was doing. My friend told me that under the Privacy Act of 1974, agencies are forbidden from maintaining any record describing how any individual exercises his or her rights guaranteed by the First Amendment unless expressly authorized by law. He asked me if the staff at the Texas Board of Professional Engineers has ever even heard of the First Amendment to the United States Constitution, or of the protections of due process.

"I told him how it is supposed to work. First, a valid complaint is sent to the accused for a rebuttal statement. If the executive director requires additional information before referring the matter to the Board for its decision, the director may request it directly from the complainant or through a staff investigation. Violations that may warrant suspension or revocation of a license must be handled under the due process procedures for a public hearing as required by the Administrative Procedure and Texas Register Act. A proposed reprimand will require less-formal proceedings, but in either case the respondent will be afforded the opportunity to show compliance with all requirements of law and defend himself against any punitive action. I told my friend I believed that the Texas Board of Professional Engineers is not only violating the engineer's First Amendment rights but also the engineer's constitutionally guaranteed rights of due process."

"Brooke," Marshal said, "if there was a member of the Board present in 2004 who was concerned about Mr. Meriano's First Amendment rights, and the same person is still sitting on the Board even now, then that means the entire Board probably knows that the staff has been violating Mr. Meriano's First Amendment rights this whole time."

"At least since March of 2004," Brooke replied. "It's the responsibility of the Board to know what the staff is doing. They are not supposed to look the other way. I've got the statute marked in this book right here. It is Section 1001.153, Division of Responsibilities: 'The board shall develop and implement policies that clearly separate the policy-making responsibilities of the board and the management responsibilities of the executive director and the staff of the board.'"

Marshal read the statute, and then Brooke said, "Here, read this letter that was written in September 2005. It's signed by the executive director himself."

Marshal read the letter aloud:

> Dear Mr. Meriano:
>
> As with many of the statutes and rules associated with our law, much is open to subjectivity, and often specific or exact listings of what constitutes a violation is up to the executive director and ultimately the Board's discretion. Certainly the section dealing with unprofessional language or correspondence is one of those rules that require such scrutiny. The Board has determined that this rule is so important that it is specified in the table of suggested sanctions for violations. The three word pairs that you referenced in the enforcement director's July 2005 dismissal notification letter were intended to make you aware of potentially questionable/marginable language that you had used in the submitted complaint.

"This says that the executive director is admitting that the rule can be interpreted subjectively," said Marshal. "Isn't there some kind of legal determination? Does any engineer know what words engineers are permitted to use or not use? Again, is the use of the word 'inflammatory' permitted for the staff to use but not permitted for the practicing engineer to use? Who's the decider of speech that some people are allowed to use but other people are not allowed to use? I've heard about sportscasters who lose their jobs because of politically incorrect speech, but just show me a list of which words in the English language the engineer is prohibited from using."

"Read on, Marshal," Brooke said.

Marshal continued reading the letter aloud:

> The enforcement director's July 2005 letter was for guidance or 'admonishment' that was stated to inform

you of concerns over stated comments that you made. My dictionary defines *admonish* as 'to warn of a fault; to reprove gently or kindly, but seriously; or to exhort; also to put one in mind of something forgotten, by way of a warning or exhortations.' The agency staff strives to assist our licensees wherever possible and the 'admonishment' was indeed to assist and guide you in your future engineering business interactions.

"So the executive director," Marshal said, "is saying that he uses a dictionary rather than a lawyer's advice? Even though the Board staff found that Mr. Meriano was not in violation of any law or rules, the executive director seems to have admitted that the staff is punishing Mr. Meriano as a result of his stated comments, violating his First Amendment rights under the U.S. Constitution. It appears that the executive director made no mention of the questionable legal basis exercised by the Board staff when it sent out a 'letter of admonishment' or 'warning.'"

"And now, Marshal," said Brooke, "I want to show you this. It's the document that you have been looking for. It's a copy of the Enforcement Detail Report that was used to damage your credibility at the arbitration hearing."

13

B rooke handed the document to Marshal. Marshal read silently and then said, "This is it. This is the document that Recker handed to me and asked me questions about. It says 'Enforcement Detail Report.' It says the file had been opened on January 14, 2005, and closed on January 27, 2005. Under 'Categories,' it says 'Residential Foundation—Repair.' Under 'Comments' it says:

> Mr. Fuelem has filed a complaint against Mr. Yeager alleging that Mr. Yeager makes grandiose, broad, and sweeping statements condemning foundations and frames for houses with little or no supporting codes to support his claims in his reports . . . It was determined that Mr. Yeager provided little information in his reports to support his opinions . . . Mr. Yeager was issued a warning that in the future he should limit his comments to the facts of the specific case and provide detailed information, calculations, and/or specific code citations to support his opinions and recommendations.

"Where did you get this, Brooke? What does it mean?"

"I found it on the computer that keeps track of complaints filed against engineers. These computer files are accessible to anyone in the agency, and they can be altered at any time. There is no name, signature, or other control mechanism that tells you or me who typed the report. For all I can tell, anyone could have typed it; however, because it is on file electronically, it might be possible for a state computer expert to retrieve the information from the computer backup files and determine exactly who typed these words. I would regard the person who typed those words as Suspect Number One.

"This report," continued Brooke, "is the only record concerning the complaint that normally remains after three years because the complaint was closed. Because it's the only record of the incident, it represents the official finding of the Texas Board of Professional Engineers, which makes you appear unworthy to even be practicing engineering, much less testifying at trials or arbitrations. On the surface, if I were an employer seeking to hire you for anything, even as an hourly employee, and I received a copy of this report, I would say that it doesn't matter how smart, skilled, or ethical you are. It's just that after reading this I simply don't think that I would want to hire you, and I would just look at the next equally qualified applicant sitting out in the office waiting for an interview. Whoever prepared this report obviously intended to deprive you of your livelihood and wreck your life."

"But it's false," protested Marshal. "I wasn't even allowed to defend myself. The Texas Board of Professional Engineers didn't even tell me that Fuelem had filed a complaint until after it was over."

"Don't worry, Marshal," Brooke said. "The perpetrators of this crime, and a 'crime' is what I will call it, were not as smart as they thought they were, and they slipped up. Dishonest people always do, especially when dealing with state agency internal politics. The vast majority of state employees are honest and know who among them are the bad apples trying to mess up the agency and their jobs. The problem in some state agencies is whether or not the bad-apple culture contaminates almost everyone else in the agency. I don't think that's the case here. I told you earlier that I found your records because someone had slipped up and the records had not been destroyed. I told you that because the Texas Board of Professional Engineers destroys its files on a complaint after three years and only the

Enforcement Detail Report remains. Quite frankly, I think somebody at the agency intentionally prevented the records from being destroyed in a concealed effort to help you. I have the rest of the records right here.

"The obvious intention by the perpetrators was to prevent you from knowing of the existence of this Enforcement Detail Report until it was too late for you to submit an open records request for all the underlying information. That is the reason that the Board's Web site contains false information when it states that an effort will be made to inform the engineer whenever someone seeks records on the engineer. But someone else is obviously compiling these falsehoods and posting them on the agency's Web site. I'll call that person Suspect Number Two.

"Normally," continued Brooke, "everything about a complaint is kept in a large paper file and then after three years, the records are destroyed in compliance with agency document destruction policies. As part of the process, usually the enforcement director or someone high up in the agency will take the file, summarize it, and put it on the Enforcement Detail Report at some time after the case has been closed. It is normally summarized in conjunction with the actual closing of the file. Then after three years the paper file is destroyed, and the Enforcement Detail Report serves as the official record of the complaint.

"There are several procedures in place that are intended to protect the engineer from being falsely accused, so someone went to extraordinary effort to destroy your reputation and career with this particular report. One requirement of the staff is to declare the claim frivolous or valid. Another requirement is to report the details of every complaint to the full Board but redact the personal identification information and make sure the details are not provided to anyone outside the agency, even under an open records request. None of that was done in your case."

Then Brooke reached down into her briefcase and pulled out several more documents.

"Fuelem did file a complaint against you in retaliation, and it says so in these staff notes. The date of Fuelem's complaint is December 9,

2004. The agency received the complaint on December 28, 2004, determined that the complaint was retaliation, and the enforcement director marked it 'dismissed' on December 30, 2004. There's no record of them even telling you that they had opened it and then closed it. But one thing is certain, Fuelem's complaint against you was definitely dismissed by the agency on December 30, 2004.

"Here's a copy of the letter you received concerning the complaint. It has an official Texas Board of Professional Engineers letterhead. The date is January 27, 2005, telling you that Fuelem filed a complaint against you and you were being issued a warning."

Marshal read the letter aloud:

> Mr. Fuelem alleged that your statements in the report were based upon unsubstantiated and/or unsupported information reflecting a lack of objectivity. Our expectations are that you will effect changes to your standard of practice in the future.

"I think I remember seeing this," said Marshal, "but I never could figure out what report they were talking about. They reference a report concerning a client unrelated to the case involving Fuelem, and there's no way Fuelem could have accessed the report that I recall. I also remember thinking that the agency has no concept of due process because they waited until after they closed the case before even telling me that a complaint had been filed. The text in this letter is certainly less offensive than the text that is provided in the Enforcement Detail Report."

"I know," said Brooke. "They sent you an inoffensive letter so that you would not be alerted to what they were up to. The text in the Enforcement Detail Report is certainly more disparaging of your reputation than the letter they sent to you."

"Then where did they get the text that they used in the Enforcement Detail Report?" asked Marshal.

"They got the wording directly from the complaint that Fuelem had dated on December 9, 2004. It is the same one that was dismissed on December 30, 2004. Here it is."

Marshal read Fuelem's original handprinted complaint. Fuelem had written the complaint on a piece of paper that contained a TFE letterhead and had signed the complaint.

"You're right," Marshal said. "The complaint language matches the language in the Enforcement Detail Report. The Board staff did not send me a copy of Fuelem's actual complaint either."

"Now look at this letter," Brooke said, "that the Board staff sent to Fuelem on January 14, 2005, after they officially closed the complaint on December 30, 2004. It says:

> Dear Mr. Fuelem:
> This is to acknowledge receipt of the complaint you have filed with the Texas Board of Professional Engineers against Mr. Yeager. The information you have provided will be evaluated by the staff. It may be necessary for us to write and ask for clarification or additional information.

"But Fuelem did not send anything to them after he had filed his initial complaint on December 9, 2004. Also, note the file number on the letter from the Board to Fuelem. Then compare it to the file number on his complaint that was dismissed on December 30, 2004. Then compare it to the file number on the Enforcement Detail Report."

"They're the same file number," said Marshal.

"Note the signature on the January 14, 2005, letter to Fuelem," Brooke continued. "And note who typed it. One of those people is high up in the agency. That person is Suspect Number Three. The other one is a person who has been slandering your name to the public. That person is Suspect Number Four."

"What do you mean, slandering my name to the public?" Marshal asked Brooke.

"There is a witness at the agency who will help you. This witness overheard a conversation that someone called the Board office with an angry tone in his voice and demanded to know whether or not he should file a complaint against you and inquired about your reputation.

Suspect Number Four told that person that you had fifteen complaints filed against you and that the agency was investigating two more."

"Go on, Brooke," said Marshal.

"Evidently you had gotten into a debate with a local well-known environmentalist during an Austin City Council meeting concerning a report that the environmentalist had written. He was still angry when he called the Board asking about you, but he decided not to file a complaint against you because he recognized you had the right to say what you did. Suspect Number Four was very upset that the environmentalist refused to file a complaint.

"The agency can create complaints, as they did to Mr. Meriano. Or they can accept complaints from other engineers, as they did to you. But their mission is supposed to be to protect the general public and not protect the financial interests of your opponents in court. It looks much better for them when they face the Texas Legislature during sunset hearings, to be able to show that they have been able to generate at least one complaint from a member of the general public against an engineer. It makes them seem relevant.

"Also, there was an earlier incident involving Suspect Number Four. Apparently during the Sandra Bullock trial, the builder's lawyer called you 'unprofessional.' Do you remember that?"

"Yes, I do," said Marshal. "I haven't thought about that in a long time."

"Somebody else also caught it," said Brooke. "It turned out that someone associated with the builder or with the builder's lawyers called the agency. Suspect Number Four spoke to that person and told him or her that the Board regarded you as unprofessional.

"And just compare the names and initials at the bottom of each of the January 14, 2005, and January 27, 2005, letters," continued Brooke. "You've got the same state employee who declared that the complaint was dismissed on December 30, 2004, signing the letter to you dated January 27, 2005. That makes that person Suspect Number Five. And there are the initials of Suspect Number Three and also Suspect Number Four, who were both copied on the January 27 letter."

"Brooke, what would make five state employees corrupt themselves to create these documents?" asked Marshal.

"Marshal, I hate to tell you this, but it looks like it's not a case of what would make them do this, it's how much were they paid to do this."

"There is another possibility," said Marshal. "We know that the governor's office complies with the demands of the homebuilding industry. There's a time gap here. The complaint was dismissed on December 30, 2004, and then resurrected on January 14, 2005, and several members of the staff then took it and ran with it. So what happened between those two dates to force the staff to change their minds and decide to reopen the complaint?"

"For one thing," said Brooke, "you can be assured that your involvement in the Sandra Bullock trial was being widely discussed by homebuilders and also people associated with the Texas Board of Professional Engineers. There could have been a telephone call from a Board member friendly to homebuilders to the staff, or even a telephone call from the governor's office itself instructing the staff to do what they are ordered to do or begin looking for another job.

"Marshal," Brooke continued, "the people at the agency know that you have never had any real complaints filed against you. They certainly know that you have never been disciplined by any state board, but Suspect Number Four was told by the higher-ups in the agency to do and say whatever it took to get a member of the general public to file a complaint against you. All of the five suspects are just regular state staff employees. Someone higher than them would had to have been compromised by some awfully powerful people. Now that I think about it, it really is possible that the jobs of those five suspects were threatened by a higher-up if they didn't do what they had been ordered to do."

Bill Kamaka had been sitting quietly during the exchange between Marshal and Brooke, listening to what was being said while reading the documents for himself.

"Marshal, Brooke, look at this," Bill said. "I just noticed something in this January 27, 2005, 'mild' letter that the staff sent to Marshal. The letter makes reference to a single report, but the Enforcement Detail Report that was closed on the same day implies that two or more reports were involved, using the plural 'reports.' Fuelem also uses the word 'reports' in his complaint. The Enforcement Detail Report bears no official state letterhead, and of course, neither does Fuelem's complaint. Fuelem's complaint actually bears the letterhead of TFE. The official document is the January 27, 2005, letter that bears the letterhead of the Texas Board of Professional Engineers, and that letter refers to the word 'report' in the singular sense.

"Think about this for a minute," Bill suggested. "The use of the word 'reports' in the plural sense is intended to criticize all of the foundation and superstructure frames that you have ever reported on, not just the single structure referenced in the January 27 letter."

"Well," Brooke said, "my lawyer friend thinks that a lawyer drafted the words used in both the complaint and the Enforcement Detail Report. Here's a letter from him that he asked me to pass on to you."

Marshal took the letter and read aloud:

> Dear Mr. Yeager:
> I understand that you attended an arbitration hearing in which that Enforcement Detail Report that Brooke has found was presented. There are several applicable evidentiary rules at play here. A judge can take judicial notice of 'learned treatises' pursuant to Section 803(18) of the Texas Rules of Evidence. TRE 803(18) is also a way to get around a hearsay objection. The arbitrator may have found the Enforcement Detail Report admissible on the fact that you authenticated it by acknowledging that a complaint had been filed against you. The arbitrator may have also admitted the document under the theory that it is a public record or self-authenticating. Then you have another rule dealing with impeachment of witnesses. The rules of evidence are not as strict in dealing with evidence used solely to impeach a witness. A judge or arbitrator has a great deal of latitude in determining what evidence is relevant and admissible. Again, this is especially true when you are dealing with impeachment. It's the judge that gets to decide what evidence is relevant and

admissible regardless of how strong your argument is to have it excluded.

In other words, an expert witness's testimony, like yours, may be rebutted by a learned treatise, sometimes to the detriment of his or her reputation. In the law of evidence, a learned treatise is a text that is sufficiently authoritative in its field to be admissible as evidence in a court in support of the contentions made. Under the common law, such evidence is considered hearsay and is not admissible except to rebut the testimony of an opposing expert witness.

In order to introduce the document into evidence, the arbitrator might have been able to take judicial notice of the text if it had been sufficiently notable that the average person would know that it is an authority. In this case, there was no letterhead or signature, and no mention of the Texas Board of Professional Engineers.

Instead, it is evident to me that the arbitrator took another approach. Another way to introduce such evidence is to adduce testimony by the expert admitting that the "text is an authority in the field." It is my understanding that in this case, the matter involving Mr. Fuelem had involved a complaint to the Board. The text had mentioned "foundations," and the subject of the DeBarberie matter that you were testifying about did include the needed repairs to their concrete foundation. The fact that Mr. Fuelem had retaliated against you was irrelevant.

Based on your testimony, without the opposing lawyer, Mr. Recker, having to actually admit the document into evidence, the arbitrator was then able to deduce that the document was authentic. He then had cause to believe that the Texas Board of Professional Engineers has officially declared that you are a disreputable professional engineer and unfit to be writing engineering reports "condemning foundations and frames" for houses with little or no supporting codes to support your claims in your reports, and that your "reports provided little information to support" your opinions.

Brooke has shown me a copy of the complaint that Mr. Fuelem filed against you. Those words appear to have been transferred directly to the Enforcement Detail Report, and it is my understanding that the same complaint was dismissed on December 30, 2004. I feel very strongly that the author of those words in the complaint as well as in the Enforcement Detail Report was not an engineer but instead was a lawyer. Most likely the lawyer dictated the words to Mr. Fuelem to write in his complaint.

"Bernie Rothenstein!" shouted Marshal.

"Who?" Brooke and Bill said in unison.

"Bernie Rothenstein," said Marshal again. "No engineer I have ever met has the ability to use words with such legal foresight, certainly not Fuelem. No, those words crafted in Fuelem's complaint were the words of a lawyer who wanted to wreck my future and the legal outcome of any lawsuit brought by any client of mine wanting to use me as an expert witness. I often testify for homebuyers instead of homebuilders, and the lawyer who wrote those words, Bernie Rothenstein, is a lawyer who works for homebuilders. As far as I am concerned, Bernie Rothenstein is a murderer," Marshal said.

"A murderer?" Bill asked. "Marshal, what are you talking about?"

"A man died because of what Rothenstein did! Now I remember what happened! Brooke, correct me if I am wrong, but in 2001, Governor Rick Perry signed a bill into law that placed the Texas Board of Professional Engineers on SD-SI status, which is an acronym for self-directed, semi-independent. Beginning in 2002, the pilot project removed the Board from the legislative appropriations process, allowing the Board to operate under its own discretion, outside the spending limitations set in the General Appropriations Act. That means they run their agency like a business, off-budget. They have to fund their agency from their revenues, and those revenues are derived from engineers' license fees and as many fines as they can levy. They then send a large percentage of those revenues to the state's general operating fund. It's profitable for the agency to assess fines against as many engineers as it possibly can. It might even be a bounty system, with some of the state employees at the top of the agency getting bonuses based on the number of complaints processed."

"I'm not sure about the bonus system, Marshal," Brooke said. "I know that I have not received a bonus, but I don't know how the higher employees at the agency are paid."

"As you have proven, Brooke," Marshal went on, "beginning in 2004 the Board implemented a policy to discipline professional engineers based on what the engineers said in depositions or wrote in their engineering reports. Selected engineers who testified in court against homebuilders and insurance corporations were targeted by the Board. The first known instance of an engineer being targeted in this manner occurred in March 2004, when attempts to discipline engineer Meriano failed because both the lawyer for the attorney general's office, as well as a Board member who is a lawyer, advised the Board staff to drop all charges against Meriano because the staff was violating his First Amendment rights. At the same time, the Executive Director Chinn was most likely forced out of state employment, apparently over the Bonfire issue.

"Now, with Ms. Chinn's replacement running the staff under their new procedures, the Board staff can solely prosecute all complaints without any Board member being the wiser, so long as the respondent to the complaint does not take it to the informal conference stage. So if the staff institutes or participates with outsiders in processing a bogus complaint such as 'unprofessional language' and extorts a fine out of the engineer before the informal conference stage, then they can supplement their revenue with administrative penalties assessed against the unfortunate licenseholder, who has no acceptable defense to such an undefined violation. Again, no one on the Board is the wiser. We're talking about possibly hundreds of Texas professional engineers under attack by the Board, and millions of dollars in licensing fees and fines.

And earlier this year, one Board member, who is evidently an accountant, suggested the fines be increased to $100,000 per incident because that's what the Texas accounting board now assesses accounting firms.

"Remember, Salven did not even try to file a complaint against Meriano in order to get the staff to start to persecute him. Salven's lawyer did that by sending deposition documents to the staff in an e-mail message, and the staff did the rest on its own without any kind of formal complaint. So now we have a track record beginning as early as March 2004 of the Board staff cooperating with a lawyer outside the agency in order to get the state to do the bidding of a corporate entity, a homebuilder, or insurance company, and try to discipline Meriano for something that he said.

"Early in 2004, I had as clients Mrs. Cathy Dickerson and Mr. James Dickerson. I asked Mrs. Dickerson to get the files on her new house from City Hall. She found a certification letter signed by the engineer who designed the foundation that indicated the engineer had designed it for low soil expansion. Then I hired a geotechnical engineer named Edward Sachem, P.E., who discovered that the soils were highly expansive, and I issued a report about that for all to see in early March 2004. Then there was a mediation held on that case. The name of the mediator was Fred Logan.

"Also," Marshal added, "the same Fred Logan who was the arbitrator in the DeBarberie lawsuit that took place a few years later—the one where Recker, the lawyer working for a contractor named Sline, presented the Enforcement Detail Report. Anyway, the mediation concerning the Dickerson house turned into something of a blowup. The mediator sent two contractors, Fuelem, and me out into another room to see if we could settle the matter amicably. When we got to the room, the four of us started to discuss the matter when Fuelem suddenly exploded at me in a fit of rage, saying, "Do you even know what you are talking about?" The other three of us looked at each other and tried to calm Fuelem down. It was pretty obvious that he was badgering and trying to get me to react, but I took it all in stride. Besides he knew that the foundation was defective, and he knew that I knew. One of the contractors asked me after the meeting to file a complaint, but because the lawsuit was already underway, I decided that I would do that later.

"A few days before Fuelem vented his rage at me, he called Dan Drapere, P.E., the engineer who had designed the foundation and told him about Edward Sachem's test results. Fuelem demanded that Dan Drapere change his certification with the city by removing the record that said the soil was of low expansiveness and replacing it with a new record that said the soil exhibited high expansive qualities. Fuelem tried to entice Drapere, telling him that if he made the change, then Fuelem would testify that Drapere's foundation design was correct, and Drapere would get more money. If Drapere didn't make the change, Fuelem threatened him saying that GrandTex Pacific would file suit against Drapere for underdesigning the foundation for the site. In effect, Fuelem was urging Dan Drapere to falsify a public document that would be entered into the city records in an effort to defraud the Dickersons and any subsequent purchasers."

"Was Fuelem doing this on his own, or was the builder's lawyer helping him?" Bill asked.

"The builder's lawyer was Bernie Rothenstein, and yes, he was in on it," Marshal said. "Drapere typed a new certification and sent it to Fuelem, who gave it to Rothenstein. Rothenstein then sent a letter to the Dickersons' lawyer, telling him something like, 'We do not agree that the foundation is failing or was defectively engineered.' But Rothenstein waited to send a copy of the changed certification to the Dickersons' lawyer until several months later, and that lawyer sent a copy of Rothenstein's letter to me."

"Did Fuelem ever enter the changed certification into the records at City Hall?" Bill asked.

"No. After all of that happened, I received a telephone call from Cathy Dickerson. She and her lawyer's paralegal had visited City Hall together. They told me that all of the records pertaining to Cathy's house were missing from the file, and when Cathy asked to replace them with copies of the records that they had given to her months before, they told her they could not do that. They needed the original documents. No one at the city knew who had taken the records."

"Did the records ever show up again?" Bill asked.

"No," Marshal said. "Cathy went by several months later to see if they were there. They were completely gone."

"I guess that means that because they did not file the changed certification with the city records, they could say that no crime had been committed," Bill said.

"Well," said Marshal, "Fuelem eventually testified that the changed certification that he held in his hand from Dan Drapere was valid. Even though he did not enter it into the city records, he was able to testify that Drapere had designed the foundation correctly because the changed document stated that Drapere had used the right numbers for a highly expansive clay soil. That might be considered to be perjury, but it would take a lawyer to figure it all out."

"What about the builder?" asked Bill. "Was he involved?"

"It doesn't look like he was involved," Marshal said. "In fact, when the builder's representative saw what Rothenstein and Fuelem were up to, he wanted to get as far away from both of them as he possibly could. Altering a public document is a crime. He didn't want to go to prison and evidently believed that those two were on their way to wearing orange prison garb. The same builder settled almost immediately after that with another client of mine."

"What about the Dickersons?" Bill asked. "What happened to them?"

"Well," Marshal replied, "Fuelem had to give a deposition, and the Dickersons' lawyer asked Fuelem a lot of questions about his involvement in changing the certification at the city. Cathy was sitting in during that deposition, but I wasn't there. Then the deposition concluded, and everyone started to leave. The lawyers went into another room to discuss the case, leaving Cathy and Fuelem alone together. Then Fuelem verbally abused her—badgered her—telling her things that she did not want to repeat to me. She called me shortly after it happened. Cathy was crying and angry, and she did not want to tell me what he had said."

"What did you do then?" Brooke asked.

"Filed a complaint," Marshal said. "Cathy did not want to file a police report. She said she was afraid of him and that he might come by the house sometime when her husband was away and seek revenge because he knew where she lived. I can't stand men who abuse women. But the law seems to state that an engineer should try to work things out first with the offending engineer before filing a complaint, so I asked Cathy what she wanted me to do. I needed to know if what he had said to her was severe enough for me to file the complaint or would she accept a simple apology from Fuelem. She said that she had spoken with her husband and that they would accept an apology. But if he wouldn't apologize, I should tell Fuelem that I would file the complaint, and they would testify at the Texas Board of Professional Engineers against him.

"So I sent a letter to Fuelem's house. I didn't want anyone at his office to see that I was about to report him to the Board, and I didn't even mention the case that both of us had been working on. I just asked him to apologize to Cathy and her husband. About two weeks later, Fuelem sent a response back to me. I could see that he had gotten with Rothenstein and the two of them had drafted the response, even though Rothenstein had clearly made pains to make it sound like Fuelem had written the letter. I remember finding a fax transmittal somewhere showing that Fuelem had faxed a copy of my letter to Rothenstein with the comment that my letter made reference to the case that he is working on with GrandTex Pacific, which was a false statement. Fuelem's letter to me said something like, 'I do not intend to issue an apology to the Dickersons notwithstanding your threat of filing a complaint with the Board.'"

Brooke interrupted. "Doesn't he understand that the law requires an engineer to file a complaint in such an instance? If you can't work it out and you don't follow up with a complaint, the Board could sanction you, Marshal."

"That's one reason I believe that Fuelem might have been under the control of Rothenstein. I think Rothenstein already knew that Joe Tuel was one of the favored engineers at the Texas Board of Professional Engineers. Dick Fuelem works for Tuel, and both work together on behalf of homebuilders. Plus, Fuelem's complaint was written on a piece of paper bearing a TFE letterhead. I am beginning to think now that Fuelem deliberately abused Cathy, hoping I would file a complaint. No engineer would take a chance like that with the

Board unless he already knew that the Board wouldn't do anything about it."

"What do you mean he was under the control of Rothenstein?" Bill asked.

"Rothenstein knew that Fuelem, Rothenstein's own expert witness, had been in the process of committing a crime by changing the certification so that he could refile it at the city. Of course Rothenstein might have been manipulating him, just setting him up so that Rothenstein could get him under control. When we finally got to the arbitration, Rothenstein had both Fuelem and Tuel walk into that arbitration hearing and perjure themselves about that certification. After I testified at the arbitration, I then filed the complaint against Fuelem. I also gave the agency staff the name of two witnesses who had seen what Fuelem had done to Cathy. Cathy and her husband told me later that no one from the Board ever called them asking for their side of the incident. With regard to my complaint against Fuelem, I never found out what happened because I never heard back from the Board."

"I think I know what happened," Brooke said. "I have a copy of a letter right here that the enforcement officer sent to Fuelem, with no copy to be sent to you. The letter says that Fuelem had not done anything wrong."

She handed the letter to Marshal who studied it for a few moments. "You're right," said Marshal. "It doesn't look like they even telephoned Cathy to ask her what happened. This letter totally ignores Fuelem's assault on Cathy. They say to Fuelem 'although the allegations may reflect unprofessional conduct, the issues did not appear to justify censure of your license.' This letter was sent on October 29, 2004.

"Here is what happened," Marshal continued. "We know that Fuelem and Rothenstein were working together at the time that Fuelem sent that letter to me, refusing to apologize for what he had said to Cathy Dickerson. Then there was the arbitration hearing where Fuelem perjured himself about the foundation certification document with Rothenstein controlling Fuelem. Then we have Rothenstein, not Fuelem, who crafted the words in the complaint making reference to 'foundations and frames,' knowing that is all we deal with in these house cases—foundations like those that TFE designs all the time and frames which comprise the wood walls, floors, and roof superstructures of houses.

"It would take a lawyer like Rothenstein, not an engineer like Fuelem, to know how to craft a document for future use that would have an adverse affect on my credibility with any future arbitrator or judge. Rothenstein could smuggle the agency's Enforcement Detail Report to the arbitrator, under the table, in any case in which I testify in the future when both he and Fuelem are involved. My clients would spend all of their money trying to take their case to arbitration, and then Rothenstein or a lawyer for another homebuilder would hand the Enforcement Detail Report to the arbitrator or judge, and my clients would automatically lose their case. And then, of course, we have some people at the Texas Board of Professional Engineers who are dishonest enough to manipulate any other records, mine included, in a way to benefit the homebuilders and their lawyers.

"I have noticed that for about five years now, ever since Governor Perry started stacking the Board with his cronies, the engineer Board has been tweaking the rules in a manner that gives considerable favor to building contractors, especially homebuilders, against professional engineers and homeowners. Contractors are now using the engineering discipline process to achieve their financial objectives, including encouraging their hired engineering expert witnesses to initiate frivolous claims against those professional engineers who work on behalf of homeowners.

"Brooke, during the time you have worked at the Texas Board of Professional Engineers, are you aware of any complaint being declared by the staff to be 'frivolous'?"

"No," Brooke answered. "Not one complaint against an engineer has ever been classified as frivolous since I started working there. And I know for a fact that the Board has discussed it and has formally or informally endorsed the staff's actions. If the staff classifies a complaint as frivolous, no outsider such as a lawyer can gain access to that record, even with a subpoena. They want lawyers to get the bogus information on engineers to use at trial in order to help homebuilders and contractors.

"Once a complaint is concluded and depending on whether or not the engineer being investigated is a favored engineer, the Board then generates separate, unsigned single-page summaries and conclusions that, by innuendo, suggest the 'subject' engineer to be unprofessional or otherwise biased against the 'complainant' engineer. Lawyers then retrieve these summary reports through open records requests for use at trial. Those summaries are the Enforcement Detail Reports. This way, the homeowner's lawyer can be sandbagged at trial and the so-called 'unprofessional' or 'biased' expert can be excluded from further court proceedings during cross-examination, thereby insuring a win for the homebuilder and his or her insurance company. This is certainly not protection of the public welfare. This is a massive fraud being perpetuated by the State of Texas against its own citizens. I've heard that somewhere close to 600,000 homebuyers are now complaining to the TRCC about the poor quality of the houses that they have been sold with the vast majority constructed by the giant interstate homebuilding corporations.

"The Enforcement Detail Reports are not destroyed as part of the Board's file retention process but are archived in a Board computer and are freely available to anyone who asks. Once obtained by lawyers or others, the reports can be archived in other computers. Once the underlying Board file documents are destroyed, there is no way for the Board to undo the defamatory allegations that remain in the Enforcement Detail Report. The Report then stands as an official state document in the eyes of the court, the public, and engineers' prospective employers."

Marshal pulled up some files on his smartphone. "It looks like Rothenstein got that Enforcement Detail Report to the arbitrator in the Dickerson case. I have an old e-mail message here from my client, James Dickerson. It's dated February 16, 2005, after the Enforcement Detail Report was compiled, and it says, 'Cathy and I really appreciate all of the work that you did for us, so I'm not thrilled about asking you this. However, the arbitrator did not reimburse us for any of the work that you or Edward Sachem performed regarding the foundation. Do you think you could stand to reduce your fee a little bit? We are still over $100,000 in the hole.'

"The testimony in the Dickerson matter," Marshal continued, "was finished in September 2004. The Texas Board of Professional Engineers closed their case against me on January 27, 2005, and the arbitrator waited until the middle of February 2005 to reach his decision. I'll bet Rothenstein told the arbitrator to delay his decision until after the Texas Board of Professional Engineers had reached a decision about me.

"Rothenstein did the same thing in the Dickerson case that Sline's lawyer, Recker, did later in the DeBarberie case. Rothenstein defamed me to the arbitrator with the Enforcement Detail Report and probably told the arbitrator that he had obtained the 'official' record from the Texas Board of Professional Engineers. Of course the arbitrator in the Dickerson case would refuse to want to allow Edward and I to be paid. Edward was working for me, testing the soils, and proving that Dan Drapere had underdesigned the foundation. Of course, reading only that Enforcement Detail Report, the arbitrator would believe that I don't know anything about 'foundations and frames.' After all, that's what the Board had officially said, as far as he knew.

"Recker didn't get that Enforcement Detail Report directly from the Texas Board of Professional Engineers. He got it from another lawyer—the one, Brooke, that you told me earlier had requested my files several years ago using an open records request. And when Recker made me answer to that fraudulent Enforcement Detail Report, the end result was that the DeBarberies lost their case as well as all the money that they had given to Sline. Recker tricked the arbitrator with that fraudulent Enforcement Detail Report. The arbitrator's decision made the DeBarberies so distraught that the stress killed Angela DeBarberie's father as soon as they learned about the decision."

"Maybe Recker did not know the source of the document," Brooke suggested.

"That's no excuse!" Marshal exclaimed. "A lawyer is trained to know that the documents he provides in a case are genuine, and Recker should have sought additional information. That Enforcement Detail Report had no identification on it to indicate that it even came from the Texas Board of Professional Engineers.

"I'll agree that Rothenstein is the instigator in all of this, and he should be the one to serve the hardest time, but Recker is also responsible. As an analogy, just because Rothenstein was inside holding up the bank and he accidentally shot the teller, a crime was still committed and it doesn't make Recker any less responsible just because he was outside the bank driving the getaway car. Same is true of Tuel, Fuelem, and the dishonest state employees and members of the Texas Board of Professional Engineers. They knew what they were doing was wrong," Marshal said. "And now they will have to pay the piper. But the biggest enchilada of them all, well, who could that be? And what will happen next?"

14

The brisk chill and the dimly lit street spurred Dale Morgan to hurry rapidly along the sidewalk, his black overcoat and wide-brimmed felt hat barely protecting him from the weather. Light sleet had begun to fall as he searched for a spot and finally parked his car three blocks away. *I should have used the valet parking. It must be below freezing tonight,* he thought, v*ery unusual for early December in Austin.*

He looked at his watch and saw that it was 8:15 p.m. *I'm late. I hope they've already seated Marshal and his friends.*

Up ahead he could see the neon sign mounted to the corner of the old brick Stratford Arms building. The sign flashed the words "Bess Bistro." Sandra Bullock had opened the restaurant in Austin only two years before. As Dale crossed San Antonio Street, he glanced across West Sixth where the Miller Building stood facing the Stratford. He smiled as he looked at the third floor of the Miller Building and remembered all those documents he had carted for Marshal to research and copy for the Sandra Bullock house trial. The homebuilder's lawyers had threatened Dale with a lawsuit, but Dale had hired his own lawyer and nothing had ever come of that.

Passing the neon sign, he approached the arched canvas awning that overhung the sidewalk with its tiny twinkling Christmas lights. He walked down the steps to the front door of the restaurant and then into the completely remodeled Stratford basement that could have easily been a speakeasy or similar hideaway in the 1930s. He walked through the crowd of people waiting to be seated at their tables while removing his coat and hat.

"Good evening, Mr. Morgan," said the maitre d'. "It's good to see you again, sir. Your party arrived only a little while ago. Everything's all set for the surprise. Let me take your coat and hat, and I will accompany you to the table."

Marshal, Brooke Kamaka, and Bill Kamaka sat at a table in the far corner of the restaurant, partially shielded from view by the exposed brick walls and the paneled decorum. Marshal saw Dale approaching and waved.

"Dale," Marshal said as he rose from his chair, "I want to introduce you to Brooke Kamaka and her father, Bill Kamaka. They helped me solve my latest engineering investigation involving the Texas Board of Professional Engineers. Brooke and Bill, I want to introduce you to Dale Morgan, who helped me solve the engineering investigation involving Sandra Bullock and her homebuilder. Dale is our gracious host this evening."

Once everyone was seated again, Marshal said, "Dale, I was telling Brooke and Bill about my latest investigation in Phoenix, Arizona, but I am just now getting to the best part. I was in the Phoenix airport carrying my laptop computer case when I walked up to the first security checkpoint. I pulled out my boarding pass and showed the agent my driver's license, and the agent then smiled and said half-jokingly, 'I see you're from Texas. What do you think about that governor of yours wanting Texas to secede from the union?' I told him, 'I have several problems with Rick Perry, and I'm sure that I will never vote for him again,' and the agent then smiled and let me go on through. As I walked ahead and started to open my case and take out my computer for the security screener, the thought suddenly struck me, 'what if I had answered that I agreed with Rick Perry and that Texas should secede?' I'll bet Homeland Security would have hauled me and any other Texans standing in line with that point of view into a back room of the airport and strip-searched us right then and there, thinking we were some kind of secessionist group. I could just envision myself standing in a big room in the Phoenix airport filled with towel-clad, naked, and barefoot Texans who were Rick Perry supporters."

Everybody at the table laughed at the thought.

"Dale," Marshal exclaimed. "How did you get a reservation to dine here tonight? I've heard that people have to call days ahead to get a reservation on a weekend, especially this time of the year. This place is packed."

"I don't know." Dale replied. "After you accepted my invitation this morning, I just called and gave them my name, and they just said to come right on down this evening. I wanted to invite you and meet your two friends whom you had spoken about and celebrate a little pre-Christmas cheer."

"Well, I've got something to cheer about," Marshal said. "I want to celebrate a young woman's achievements that I heard about last week. She obtained her doctorate in biomedical engineering in spite of her severe disabilities. Her name is Brittany Anderson, the young woman I once told all of you about who was severely injured when the Aggie Bonfire collapsed. Her parents visited me several years ago and asked for some advice. They called me last week about her accomplishment, but they also wanted to tell me that Brittany had finally won her lawsuit against the administration at Texas A&M. Her lawyer and the Texas attorney general's office finally settled her case, and now she can pay all of her medical bills."

"Marshal, that's great," Dale exclaimed.

"I told her parents years ago," Marshal recalled, "that I was suspicious of the role the governor's office played in all of that. My reading of Governor Perry is that with the power to veto bills and appoint members of boards and commissions, he alone is able to bypass the Texas Legislature and dictate policy throughout the entire state government. It seems like if there is a board or commission member whom he cannot control, then that board member or commissioner will be replaced. Then if Rick Perry disapproves of the activities of a particular state employee who does not obey the wishes of the Board, then the Board will find a way to push that person out of a job. For example, at the Texas Board of Professional Engineers, it is highly likely that Ms. Chinn could have been forced to resign over the Aggie Bonfire matter because she said too much to the news media, plus the fact that she was probably unwilling to persecute engineers for their manner of speech just because the engineers happened to testify against homebuilders.

"I don't know who or what is behind Governor Perry," Marshal continued, "either domestic or foreign, but a corporate homebuilder–state government partnership, like the TRCC, was beginning to look very un-American to me. I have been working with some friends who said that although the Texas Legislature has now ordered the TRCC to close, the homebuilders have promised to try to reenact it and even spread the TRCC concept to other states in conjunction with 'tort reform.' I'm concerned that some governments or corporate groups might be trying to instill a dictatorial form of government here in Texas, with an eye on spreading it to the rest of the nation. With all due respect, no Aggie could possibly come up with a plan like that all by himself."

"I don't know about the rest of you," Bill said, "but I get the impression that the governor may be some kind of chameleon. I've heard that Jason Embry, who is a reporter down at the *Austin American-Statesman,* is about to write an article that we have a 'Chamber of Commerce' Perry with nice suits for corporate groundbreakings; 'Natural Disaster' Perry with beige work shirt and jeans and a keen knowledge of the line between projecting command and spending too much time in front of the cameras; 'Tea Party' Perry, the fun governor with baseball cap and jeans, standing on the Capitol steps and shouting 'reread the Constitution'; and then we have 'Monochromatic' Perry with black shirt under black jacket, hanging around with celebrities or commanding protesters to remember Jesus's command to 'love thy neighbor.' To that I say, 'Beware of a wolf in sheep's clothing.'"

"Bill," said Dale, "Marshal told me earlier today that you are a tenured professor of civil engineering, so your future might be reasonably secure. But for those of us in the private sector we have really gotten hurt by the corporate–state government partnership here in Texas, particularly in the form of the TRCC. I am an investor and have lost about half of what little wealth I had thanks to the latest collapse in the stock market. Marshal here told me about how the TRCC delayed the resolutions between homebuilders and homebuyers in Texas, and now that the economy has gone into the dumper, the large builders have either filed for bankruptcy or are moving back out of state. I wish I had listened to Marshal's warnings years ago.

"Many of the original owners of those major homebuilding corporations," continued Dale, "sold most of their stock holdings beginning last year leaving the rest of us stockholders in a lurch. State laws have made the Texas homebuilding industry a magnet for unscrupulous builders. This state allowed and even encouraged substandard construction and tort reform, which I predict will destroy the life savings of countless Texas homebuyers and cause the demise of entire housing subdivisions. It may have already contributed to the nationwide economic collapse. All of the large national homebuilders operating in Texas owned their own mortgage companies. Most even owned title and insurance companies and enjoyed cozy relationships with subcontractors, material suppliers, inspectors, engineers, and realtors. This type of vertical integration created a conflict of interest here, allowing substandard homes and subprime loans to feed a residential construction conglomerate, while Texas laws tipped the scales of justice in favor of builders rather than consumers.

"Just the other day, a friend of mine who is a significant investor in a New York investment group showed me a letter that he had received from that particular investment group. The letter referred to the fact that the collapse of the housing and mortgage markets has destroyed billions of dollars in shareholder value at the nation's homebuilders. It said that investors in a Fort Worth–based national homebuilder had lost $3.5 billion in one year alone. The letter made reference to the fact that the large homebuilders may not merely be casualties of the crisis, referring I think to the fact that they might have actually caused the crisis.

"The letter pointed out that as a result of improper business practices particularly within their mortgage affiliates, several of the nation's largest homebuilders may, in fact, be complicit parties in causing the industrywide collapse. It also said that the federal and state authorities have stepped up enforcement of existing law and are considering new regulations on homebuilders and mortgage originators. The letter also referred to an apparent culture of noncompliance that has exposed homebuilders and mortgage originators to extensive litigation alleging illegal practices, and that many large homebuilders have been sued by homebuyers and shareholders so far this year. I particularly remember how the letter closed. It said that the Fort Worth homebuilder is at a critical juncture financially and that the collapse of the housing and mortgage markets had not only decimated the company's earnings and share price, it had also exposed the company and its shareholders to considerable legal, regulatory, and reputation risk."

"I'm sorry to ramble about all that," Dale said. "Brooke, I hope I didn't bore you."

"Not at all, Dale," Brooke said. "As everybody at this table knows, this nation is in debt to China. What will happen if the Chinese government tells the United States to pay up at this point in time? A time in which we have sent our young men and women off to fight two wars to protect the suppliers of petroleum to this country; protect treasonous American corporations that are covertly receiving over $100 billion in contract payments, loans, and grants from American taxpayers to help Iran with its nuclear program and development of its oil and gas reserves; and protect the supply of opiates to the international corporate drug industry so that our 'government,' not our 'country,' can perpetuate the military–industrial complex and require our military to become the policemen of the world. I'm thinking that China might actually have wanted to make money in the global market to benefit many of its own citizens. Now there is the possibility that China could use its U.S. Treasury bond holdings as a weapon against us. And Iran seems to be governed by isolationists."

"Brooke, it sounds like you and I might think alike," said Dale.

The waiter came over to the table and took everyone's dinner orders. Dale ordered a bottle of merlot for the table.

"Brooke," said Marshal, "you have reminded me of something that took place during the trial of Sandra Bullock versus her homebuilder. I was still on the witness stand after the judge had excused the jury. As all of us are probably aware, Sandra Bullock is a celebrity throughout most of the world. During my testimony, I saw a very well-dressed Chinese gentleman sitting quietly in one of the spectator rows with some other similarly attired men on his left, right, and behind him. He seemed to be listening to my testimony very intensely. It was such a small courtroom that I had spotted him while I was testifying. Then during the break, the trial judge introduced the man to the trial participants and the spectators to be a judge of high importance in China, equivalent in importance to a judge who sits on our United States Supreme Court. The man and three of his associates followed me out of the courtroom after I had completed my testimony, but they didn't say anything to me.

"I didn't even think about it until just now. It was apparent that not only were stories about the trial being published in newspapers and magazines in the United States and Europe but probably also in China which, as we all know now, has become increasingly worried about the amount of national debt and trade imbalance that our United States government has accumulated through its irresponsible tax-and-spend policies. The trial had already alerted powerful people internationally to the fraud taking place in the homebuilding industry in Texas as well as in much of the rest of the nation.

"That trial occurred in late 2004," continued Marshal, "and by then I was becoming deeply enmeshed in helping clients deal with homebuilders. I saw how it would be next to impossible for them to resell their homes. What that means to a lender of money is that the collateral securing the loan is worthless, and I'll bet the Chinese government was only just then beginning to realize the impact, on their own economy, of all the fraudulent homebuilding scams that were taking place here. What country in its right mind is willing to loan money to the United States when our own government turns a blind eye to all the fraud and kickbacks? And there is no doubt in my mind that the United States government, and certainly the Texas government, knew what was taking place within the homebuilding industry."

"Marshal," Brooke said, "I'm no longer with the Texas Board of Professional Engineers since I blew the whistle on them. I'm working with a local environmental engineering firm now, so I've lost track of what's happened at the Board. Whatever happened to those people who caused your client's death?"

"You're speaking about Howard Erickson," Marshal said. "I'm still horrified about that. Dale, you haven't heard this story, but I will make it brief. A superlawyer named Bernie Rothenstein was in league with major homebuilders plus two crooked engineers, Joe Tuel and Dick Fuelem, who designed those gosh-awful stressed steel cable foundation systems. Rothenstein was also in league with a small number of dishonest state employees and Board members at the Texas Board of Professional Engineers. They all conspired together to create a fraudulent document about me so that homebuilders could win their cases when the cases went before arbitrators. What they did to me should be a warning to everyone whose livelihoods are subject to state licensing – engineers, medical doctors, even barbers. It's a warning that licensed professionals can be denied due process and prevented from legally working when a statist regime takes over a democracy. In other words, if you work without your license, you can go to jail; and if you don't work, the state can arbitrarily cut off your government safety net and literally starve you to death. Basically, the state tried me, convicted me, and figuratively executed me before even telling me that I was under investigation, which shows the power of the corporate state over the individual citizen that we now have in Texas. This is all thanks to Rick Perry, who even tried to force young girls to subject themselves to mandated immunizations that apparently would benefit a large drug corporation. It took the entire Texas Legislature to stop him, and the average voter doesn't even have a clue what's going on. Anyway, the end result of what the state did to me was that my client, Howard Erickson, became so distressed by the outcome of the arbitration and the impact on his daughter, that he died almost immediately after hearing the results. Brooke and Bill helped me learn the identities of the perpetrators. I have turned all of the records over to the district attorney's office, and they said that they would handle it from there. They also have a public integrity unit that investigates state officials, and there are several state officials I am asking them to investigate. I also intend to go before a judge and ask that the court seize the personal assets of the perpetrators and distribute those assets to all my homeowner victims who were defrauded by the use of that document. Frankly, I think every homebuyer in Texas who was swindled by the homebuilders working together with the TRCC should claim the personal assets of the perpetrators. But I intend to concentrate only on trying to help my own clients."

"What did the D.A.'s office say would happen to this superlawyer?" Dale asked.

"Bernie Rothenstein? That guy is an elitist, and they think that he will get away with it. He's saying he didn't have any idea what Tuel and Fuelem were up to even though Fuelem is screaming that Rothenstein owes him money. Also, he's got a lot of political and corporate contacts in Washington who need him to advance their own globalist agendas and who are going to work very hard to make sure that he stays licensed as a lawyer and out of jail. I'm almost certain that he and I met sometime in the past, and something about him makes me think that one day in the future his path and mine will probably cross again."

"What are you going to do about that false Enforcement Detail Report floating around from lawyer to lawyer?" asked Brooke.

"As to the document itself, I now know that it and other false documents are circulating through law firm computers throughout the state and probably throughout the nation. So, I am in the process of asking a judge to expunge the documents from the state record and also to give me a document that I can give to my lawyer-clients, saying in effect that the fraudulent document and similar documents produced by the Texas Board of Professional Engineers are untrue and are to be disregarded.

"Now all of you, it's Christmas in about two weeks," Marshal exclaimed as he opened a shopping bag that he had carried into the restaurant. "Dale, you know that in addition to books and sports, I also enjoy good movies. So in appreciation for you steering me to Sandra Bullock's house case and inviting us down to Bess Bistro tonight, I'm giving you a DVD that features Sandra Bullock. The movie is titled *Crash*. In the past, you've mentioned to me your concerns about your parents' medical care, and as you know, there is a major push toward socialized medicine now in the country. A recent poll indicates that more than half of people who say that they are

Democrats are now coming out of the closet and are admitting to wanting to live in a socialistic country, as if some of us didn't know that 40 years ago.

"There's a part in the movie involving an admittedly obnoxious policeman who is meeting with a healthcare bureaucrat in her office. The policeman pleads that his elderly father is suffering from a medical condition that is an emergency. The bureaucrat tells the policeman that if his father had come into her office that day and had spoken to her directly, instead of the policeman coming in on behalf of the father, then she might have authorized the healthcare that the father needed. But instead, because the bureaucrat harbors a personal prejudice against the policeman, she cruelly refuses medical treatment for the father and has a security guard throw the policeman out of her office. Unless you are born into the family of a politician or other member of the American corporate or political elite, that's the kind of healthcare treatment we can all expect to receive in the future if the drug corporations and the government have their way. So stay alert and when it comes, contact your representatives, and tell them to block it. And if they refuse, fire them at the polls in the next election and elect others who will promise to undo the damage.

"Bill," Marshal continued, "I'm giving you a DVD of *The Good Shepherd*. You once told me that you interviewed for a job with the CIA right after getting out of college, and this movie is a story about the birth of the CIA. Robert DeNiro's portrayal of the character General Bill Sullivan is excellent, but one line in the movie that I find particularly applicable to the Texas Board of Professional Engineers and many of the federal bureaucracies that burden all of our lives today goes something like, 'There has to be oversight. I'm concerned that too much power will wind up in the hands of too few. You know who gave Hitler his power? The clerks, the bookkeepers, the civil servants.' Just like the CIA, and now the Texas Board of Professional Engineers, all major federal and state agencies, boards, and commissions need oversight by totally independent and noncorruptible people."

"Thanks, Marshal," said Bill, who had been sitting there seemingly distracted since he had mentioned the word 'chameleon.' "What was the name of that movie that Al Pacino was in, where Lucifer morphed into different-looking people?"

"You might be thinking of *The Devil's Advocate*," said Brooke. "The character name for Lucifer was John Milton, which was the name of the British poet who wrote *Paradise Lost*."

"And Brooke," said Marshal, "I'm giving you a copy of a book by attorney Phyllis Schlafly titled *The Supremacists*. It is an excellent book about how our Constitution specifically defines *itself*, not the opinions of judges, as the 'supreme law of the land' and how political judges have twisted our Constitution into making our government into a government of men's laws and not a government of God's laws upon which our Republic was founded. For over 50 years, many political leaders of my generation have been greedy, hedonistic, and gluttonous, passing reckless and irresponsible laws. They have also passed massive debt to your generation in spite of the efforts of many good people of my generation who have tried to put a stop to it. I'm very concerned that we are about to lose this country, and your generation has got to find a way to save it while older people like Bill and I keep fighting to expose the corruption of the enemy within. There will be no such thing as retirement for me, and if you don't fight you won't be able to retire either. What we might be seeing during this time in history could be the beginning of a collapse of the so-called New World Order, which I believe has been destroying this nation since at least the late 1970s. We might also be living through the same type of economic and government collapse that occurred in Argentina, which in the early twentieth century was one of the richest and most powerful nations in the world but was brought to ruin thereafter when the government took over the economy. Your generation must fight by becoming the leaders of tomorrow, the masters of professional engineering, and honorable and creative business people who produce tangible products and services that benefit mankind.

"You might recall that I asked you to thank your lawyer friend for all the help he provided in that engineering Board matter, so you might ask him to also read Schlafly's book and see what he thinks about it. Your generation must produce ethical lawyers and judges who truly seek truth and justice, not the lies and raw power that I have seen that destroy individual creativity, our liberties, our free-trade policies, and our economy as has been happening for the last four decades. And for those people who would prefer to work with their hands in the trades, the sky's the limit if vocational schools would reopen and our government would provide the incentives to return industry and manufacturing to the nation. Vocational schools and labor unions once provided a skilled workforce with excellent training programs for people who wanted to learn a trade and who had no interest in incurring the debt of getting a college education and then finding out later that they were unhappy.

"Your generation must serve our country, if not in military service then by running for public office or simply becoming well informed before casting your vote for anyone, whether it be a campaign for the local school board, Legislature, Congress, or president of the United States. It will be up to your generation to tear down the regulatory burdens placed on American citizens at every level of government and that now engulf all of us like swarms of locusts or wood-boring termites that eat into every part of our being."

"Thanks, Marshal," Brooke said. "My appetite just went away with the locust-termite-thing. Now can we be a little more Christmas-y?"

"Okay," said Marshal. "But please let me make one last point, and then I will be done. All of us at this table are true believers in the freedoms that we Americans enjoy, and we all are willing to fight for this nation any way we can. Our country and form of government were founded on constitutional principles. Although the majority of the citizens of our country are adherents to our Constitution, the 'government' itself has gone down a different path in my lifetime, away from the constitutional principles of our nation's founders, and it is certainly no longer the government we had when I was a child. People ask me if I believe our government was behind 9/11, and I tell them that I have no opinion mainly because I don't want to be involved in conspiracy theories. I have to take time to gather and study the evidence, and if I haven't taken the time to do that, then I don't want to express an opinion. There's no doubt that Islamic terrorists hijacked and flew planes into buildings, and I am not impressed with the wild theories of people not educated in structural engineering and progressive collapse. But I don't discount other things that make me wonder why the government did certain things that day. I was in New York City at a convention that terrible morning, and I saw firsthand the obstacles that were thrown against the engineers who tried to get copies of the plans for the World Trade Center. The New York Port Authority successfully used their lawyers to block professional engineers from copying the plans of the buildings on 9/11 and continued to block the engineers for almost six months after that day. Finally we were able to get the plans from another engineering firm. So why is it that the government, in that case the New York Port Authority, moved so fast to block the engineers who were trying to find ways to help the first responders shore up the still-standing structures and search the rubble for victims and forensic evidence? Were they afraid that the engineers might find evidence of something presently unknown, such as a bomb having been detonated in the basement levels or in the subway system below the World Trade Center? Who knows, but I'm not going to assert an opinion until I believe that I have all the facts.

"I learned my lesson decades ago, which was to question every aspect of our government. I grew up in the 1950s believing that our government would never lie to us. That all changed after President Kennedy was assassinated in 1963, and we got the official story from the government that Lee Harvey Oswald acted alone. Then after the Warren Commission report, and as the military–industrial complex was gaining momentum, a number of us engineers who are detail-minded began to question various erroneous scientific missteps concerning the government's official assassination investigation. Then, only a few years ago, I saw on the History Channel a re-creation of the assassination using alleged forensic engineering techniques. Throughout the entire documentary, two words kept ringing in my mind. Those two words were 'junk science.' I then realized that the denial of government involvement in the Kennedy assassination is still going on today. So I tend to ask why. Why is it so important that the government's story about the Kennedy assassination still continues today, if for no other reason than to try to change real history? In other words, it's to distract young people into believing the government's story so that they don't question their government further. And then when the people start to ask questions, government lackeys and the mind-manipulating news media get nervous and discredit the questioners, calling them conspiracy theorists and other names. The government treats us like we're children still in grade school who must be taught certain things but not others.

"President Ronald Reagan once said, 'Freedom is never more than one generation away from extinction. We didn't pass it to our children in the bloodstream. It must be fought for, protected, and handed on for them to do the same, or one day we will spend our sunset years telling our children and our children's children what it was once like in the United States where men were free.'

"My point is this: ask questions! Force the government to answer your questions, and do not allow it to conceal itself. Be a pain to the government, organize a group if the government won't answer your questions, expose them any way you can, and stay after them. The federal and state governments are not your friends. Many unionized government agency employees and many politicians from both sides of the aisle look at you and the other taxpayers as their free meal ticket through life. Even though the Texas Legislature has now abolished the TRCC, questions remain as they close the agency, and TRCC still refuses to respond to open records requests. Whenever any government agency refuses to completely honor an open records request or to honor a request filed under the Freedom of Information Act, you know that the employees and officials in that agency are trying to cover up something illegal. The only way that the enemies of America can really undermine this country is from within our own government. Our enemies operate in the dark of night and quietness of confidentiality. Okay, Brooke, I'm officially finished with my little speech, now."

"Hey, Marshal," said Dale. "Not necessarily to raise the mood a little bit here, but speaking of termites and wood, do you remember those beautiful wormwood floors that were in Sandra Bullock's house?"

"Yes, Dale. But I don't remember termites being an issue in that house."

"No! Not termites!" exclaimed Dale, flabbergasted. "There were no termites! I'm talking about the beautiful wormwood flooring. As you probably already know, Sandra Bullock recycled almost everything and gave most of it away to charity, but she seems to have kept a little piece of it for herself. Look down at this table."

Marshal looked down at the tabletop. "You're right, Dale. This beautiful table has got to be the same wormwood floor material that we saw. She must have had it salvaged from her house and turned into tabletops. Look at the other tables around us. They are made of the same type of wood."

The waiter brought the plates of food and placed them in front of the four friends, who continued to discuss wood tables intermixed with politics.

"Excuse me, Mr. Yeager," said the wine steward, who had approached the table unnoticed. "The maitre d' informed me that you would be dining with us tonight. Please let me present you with this fine bottle of 2003 Chateau Petrus Pomerol as a gift for your dining pleasure."

"I don't understand," said Marshal. "How do you know me, and why are you giving me this gift?"

"Mr. Yeager, this bottle of wine has been stored in our wine cellar with your name on it for several years now, ever since Bess Bistro opened after you helped Ms. Bullock. We thought you might never come in to dine with us. Mr. Dale Morgan here is a regular diner, and he mentioned your name long ago. After we mentioned our dilemma to him, he called us today and told us that he would be inviting you and your friends to dinner. Our dinner reservations are usually booked two weeks in advance, but we completely rearranged our reservations and seating arrangements for this evening. In fact, we brought in the extra table where you are now seated. This wine is a present from 'a friend.'"

"I don't know," said Marshal. "People are having a pretty hard time out there right now. I don't know if I would feel right accepting it."

"Marshal, are you crazy?" said Dale. "They've gone to a lot of trouble for us this evening. If you won't accept it, then I will."

"All right," said Marshal. "I can see now that Mr. Morgan here has pulled a little surprise on me. Please pour the wine."

The wine steward poured some wine into Marshal's glass. Marshal savored its delicate, full-bodied flavor and instructed the steward to pour the wine for the others. Then when the wine was poured, the four lifted their glasses.

"A toast," Marshal said, "to Sandra Bullock, without whom I would never have started on this quest that brought me such wonderful friends. May her days be long and filled with success, love, and happiness, and to all of our days as well."

"To Sandra Bullock, and to all of us!" they all shouted. All four friends drank and savored the exquisite wine.

"Wow! That's good," said Dale. "Now let's eat."

REFERENCES AND SUGGESTED READINGS

Ahmad, Janet. "Sandra Bullock's Days in Court—Updated." http://www.hobb.org, Homeowners For Better Building Web site, September 19, 2004.

Alexandrovna, L., M. Kane, and L. Beyerstein. "The Permanent Republican Majority: Part III—Running Elections from the White House." *The Raw Story*, December 16, 2007.

Auerbach, Robert D. *Deception and Abuse at the Fed: Henry B. Gonzalez Battles Alan Greenspan's Bank.* Austin: University of Texas Press, 2008.

Austin, Christopher. "Texas PE Board Rules on Aggie Bonfire." *The Dallas Morning News*, June 15, 2000.

Berger, Raoul. *Selected Writings on the Constitution.* Cumberland, VA: James River Press & Center for Judicial Studies, 1987.

"Bob Perry: Building Homes and Candidacies." *HomeownersOfTexas.org*, September 16, 2008.

"Bonfire Collapse Texas A&M University." U.S. Fire Administration/Technical Report Series, USFA-TR-133, November 1999.

"Bonfire Suit Settlement Announcement." *Texas A&M News & Information*, October 28, 2008.

Branch, Robin G. "Standing on Shifting Ground." *Austin American-Statesman*, July 26, 1998, 1.

Copelin, Laylan. "Ruling OKs Justice's Handling of DeLay Associates' Case." *Austin American-Statesman*, January 2, 2009, A1.

"The Corporation." *HomeownersOfTexas.org*, http://www.homeownersoftexas.org/CorporateBehavior.html.

Crissey, Mike. "Engineering Board Probes Bonfire." *Laredo Morning Times*, November 24, 1999, 6A.

Dennis, Alicia, and S. Silverman. "Sandra Bullock's Texas House Trial Begins." *People*, August 20, 2004.

"District Attorney Asked to Investigate Texas Medical Board Officials."
http://www.aapsonline.org/nod/newsofday474.php, Association of
American Physicians and Surgeons Inc. Web site, November 10,
2007.

"Doctors Sue Texas Medical Board for Misconduct—Cites Institutional
Culture of Retaliation & Intimidation."
http://www.aapsonline.org/newsoftheday/004, Association of
American Physicians and Surgeons Inc. Web site, December 21, 2007.

Embry, Jason. "Which Perry Will Appear? The Right One, for Any
Situation." *Austin American-Statesman*, February 10, 2010, A5.

Embry, Jason, and K. Herman. "Texas Enterprise Fund: A&M Grant
Skirts Panel." *Austin American-Statesman*, March 27, 2009, A1.

"Engineering Express." Texas Board of Professional Engineers
Newsletter, Number 34, Summer 2007.

Goodwyn, Wade. "Did Builder's Clout Trap Couple in Dream Home?"
NPR's Weekend Edition, March 28, 2009.

Haurwitz, Ralph K. M., and L. Copelin. "Faculty Doubted Bonfire's
Stability." *Austin American-Statesman*, December 19, 1999, A1.

"Homeowners Group helps Reform State Agency,"
HomeownersOfTexas.org, 2009.

"House of Pain." *People*, November 1, 2004.

Jeffreys, Brenda Sapino. "Slow Burn." *Texas Lawyer*, November 5, 2001.

Kever, Jeannie, and M. Tolson. "Cash, Power and Tumult Within A&M."
Houston Chronicle, June 21, 2009.

Kreytak, Stephen. "Builder of Bullock Home Says He Hid Some Costs."
Austin American-Statesman, August 25, 2004.

Leef, George C. "The Supreme Court's Attacks on Freedom." January 15,
2010, http://www.campaignforliberty.com/article.php from *The Dirty
Dozen: How Twelve Supreme Court Cases Radically Expanded Government
and Eroded Freedom*, by Robert A. Levy and William Mellor (Sentinel,
2008).

Leggett, Christopher. "The Valuation of Life As It Applies to the Negligence-Efficiency Argument." *Law & Valuation*. Spring 1999.

Letter from Carole Keeton Strayhorn, Texas Comptroller of Public Accounts, to Honorable Todd Smith, Texas House of Representatives. January 23, 2006.

Lindell, Chuck. "Justice: End Judicial Elections." *Austin American-Statesman*, February 12, 2009.

"Lobbyists Spend Millions on Lawmakers." Associated Press, *Austin American-Statesman*, January 26, 2009.

"Mandatory Binding Arbitration: Unfair & Everywhere." *HomeownersOfTexas.org*.

McCormac, Jack C. *Structural Analysis*. New York: HarperCollins, 1962.

Moore, James. "Smear Artist," *Salon.com*, August 28, 2004.

Onion Creek Crawdaddies. *Irons in the Fire*. http://www.onioncreekcrawdaddies.com.

Osborn, Claire. "Actress Admits Being Slow to Question Bills." *Austin American-Statesman*, September 1, 2004.

Osborn, Claire. "Bullock House Case Goes to Jury." *Austin American-Statesman*, October 8, 2004.

Price, Asher. "New York's Waste May Make Texas a Top Dump." *Austin American-Statesman*, February 8, 2009, A1.

"Rangel: Hutchison Camps Waging Big Bucks Battle." *Lubbock Avalanche-Journal*, September 26, 2009.

"Resolution Reached on Texas A&M Bonfire." http://www.tbpe.state.tx.us, Texas Board of Professional Engineers Web site, July 26, 2002.

Riggenbach, Jeff. "Hushing Up 'Conspiracy Theories.'" http://www.campaignforliberty.com/article.php, Campaign for Liberty Web site, February 20, 2010.

Robison, Clay. "A Builder, a Commission and a Lot of Cash," *HomeownersOfTexas.org*, August 24, 2008.

Robison, Clay. "Express News Capital Update," *San Antonio Express-News*, December 15, 2008.

Rosser, Mary Ann. "Board That Disciplines Doctors May Be Reined In." *Austin American-Statesman*, April 15, 2009.

Rothbard, Murray. "The Anatomy of the State." *Rampart Journal*, 1965.

Schlafly, Phyllis. *The Supremacists: The Tyranny of Judges and How to Stop It.* Dallas: Spence Publishing, 2004.

"Special Commission on the 1999 Texas A&M Bonfire—Final Report." May 2, 2000.

Sunset Advisory Commission Report to the 78th Legislature—Texas Board of Professional Engineers.

Sunstein, Cass, and Adrian Vermeule. "Conspiracy Theories." Harvard Public Law Working Paper No. 08-03. January 15, 2008.

"Take That! Sandra Bullock Personally Helps Knock Down Her $6.5 Million Dream Home That Turned Into a Nightmare." *People*, March 27, 2006.

Texans for Public Justice. "Sun Never Sets on Politicians Taking Homebuilder Money." *Lobby Watch*, September 25, 2008.

"Texas Homebuilding and the Global Financial Collapse." *HomeownersOfTexas.org*, October 2009.

"TRCC—Time to Let the Sun Set on Bob Perry's Builder Commission." *HomeownersOfTexas.org*, May 17, 2009.

Ward, Mike. "State Senate Knocks Down Perry Parole Board Pick." *Austin American-Statesman*, May 14, 2009, A1.

"Web of Influence." *The Dallas Morning News* interactive graph, http://www.dallasnews.com/sharedcontent/dws/graphics/0109/influence/.

5077186R0

Made in the USA
Charleston, SC
26 April 2010